T0062330

The Executioner's Confession

by
Benjamin Kwakye

CISSUS WORLD PRESS

THE EXECUTIONER'S CONFESSION

Copyright © Benjamin Kwakye, 2015.

Publisher's Information & Address:

Cissus World Press

P.O. Box 240865

Milwaukee, WI 53224

www.cissusworldpressbooks.com

First published in the U.S.A by Cissus World Press

ISBN: 978-0-9679511-0-2

Cover art by Philip N. Okoro

CISSUS WORLD PRESS BOOKS are published by Dike Okoro, Founding Publisher

CONTENTS

Chapters One: The Fool's Tomatoes   5

Chapter Two: Embrace of the Shadows   21

Chapter Three: The Interview   47

Chapter Four: A Day in the Life   67

Chapter Five: Afternoon Delight   85

Chapter Six: The Executioner's Confession   91

Chapter Seven: The Glitter   115

Chapter Eight: The Farewell   131

Chapter Nine: Random Visitations and Thoughts   153

Chapter Ten: Rendezvous   163

Chapter Eleven: Of Friends and Secrets   177

Chapter Twelve: The Return   191

In loving memory to my father -

B. S. K. Kwakye

A lion who stood tall among men

Now you reside with the angels

CHAPTER ONE

***

The Fool's Tomatoes

A month after my best friend Anan died, the fog of funk that had enveloped us still wouldn't lift. Trapped in its stifling dampness, I sat in front of my home one early morning and looked over at his now desolate home, sad that his life was so prematurely snuffed by cholera. If sadness were the equivalent of tears, mine would flood oceans. I was that inconsolable even as I welcomed the sun's spitting rays descending on me as though in cruel benevolence. The cocks crowed their morning alarms and the morning pigeons and sparrows chirped their tunes, together creating a harmonious cacophony as the village rose slowly to the beat. It was as if the flowers lifted their petals (to me, their mourning hearts reddened by sadness like mine) while the morning breeze swept them into a dance of harmony. The nearby stream, drinking deep the glory of daylight, seemed to capture the sunrays as well. A beautiful morning had arrived in our village. Yet I was sad because Anan was dead.

Anan was more than a friend. He was a brother. And more. After all, he had given me gifts so priceless and selfless I almost couldn't believe he'd done it: two daughters (Ama and Abena). This had happened after I discovered that the gods, as though pulling a malevolently humorous prank, had neutralized the creative power of the juices flowing from my loins. On the insistence of family and friends, I had divorced my first wife because she was childless after five years of marriage. ("What good is a wife if she can't bear you children?" they asked. "She's a curse.")

Two years and another marriage later, however, I still didn't have children. Nor was it for lack of effort. I ate tiger nuts, chewed tree barks and drank potions designated for potency. So equipped, I was at it every night, pumping like a mad man, thinking that the stronger the thrust, the further the juices would go. No use. But my first wife had remarried and borne twins as though doubly to tease me. I concluded when her twins arrived that I was the one who'd failed to fertilize her obviously agile eggs. That discovery was so emasculating that I cursed the gods and God in equal measure and considered suicide to negate the sorry creation that I was. What were others saying when my back was turned? What use is a man if he can't implant fertile seeds in his wife?

It was Anan who rescued me from this seemingly hopeless brink. We'd been friends since childhood. And we'd grown up as brothers, fostering a relationship that seemed so well balanced, helping each other, sharing hopes, mutually condoling over each other's failures. So it was natural that my wife would go to him, rightly concerned that I would do something foolish in my depression. Anan came to see me immediately. He was that kind of person. At first, I was afraid to admit to him the cause of my despair. But patiently he waited by me and prodded gently like the elements in their constancy until my resistance eroded. At that very moment when I was rising out of my hopelessness, I knew what I must do.

7

He was a strong, handsome, virile young man and he wasn't married yet. Women swarmed, men warmed up, to him. He must be able to help me. My wife Eno thought over the proposition a long time. Then, armed with her consent, I approached Anan. "I will be honored," was all he said. It was a request I had made selfishly and I was hoping for a favorable response (although expecting a rejection). But I had underestimated his love. And so we'd allowed him into our bedroom ostensibly to sire my children. After they were born, Anan and I became even better friends, better brothers. He made no demands, never revealed the arrangement (to the best of my knowledge) and was good with the children.

His passion was farming. He kept a small farm on the outskirts of the village and would bring us some of his crops from time to time. Occasionally, he would help us on our little tomato garden in the backyard. I had never seen a man demonstrate such unbridled pride in gardening tomatoes. He often would stay for supper and it was as if the children knew he resided in them. And he kept them laughing with his endless humor and folktales. They loved him. And now Anan was dead and the children were unhappy. With his death, a novel rancor overtook us. I became easily irritated and often yelled at my wife and daughters. My wife yelled back and usually threatened me with bodily harm. My daughters recoiled into a tunnel of sadness from which they couldn't escape. It was clear we all needed Anan. But he was dead.

The day I looked over at his empty home and reminisced, I decided to do something to rebuild the family. But all day, intention and deeds traveling parallel lines, I fought with my wife and children. That evening, Eno, Ama and Abena remained indoors. I escaped this female triumvirate that suddenly seemed closed to me. It appeared they had developed their own language, which reliance on the long album of our years of intimacy couldn't decode. I stood outside hoping hopelessly.

And then, in the faded evening, a shadowy profile suddenly stood tall as a tree near my doorstep like a gift from nothingness, like an upstart come to usurp the pervasive melancholy. I peered at him in the waning discomfort of the moment, hoping for a sign. For moments, we stood facing each other, words muted by dawning recognition. There was no tension, just some uncertainty.

"How are you?" I ventured into the unbroken.

"I'm well," he replied in bass.

"May I be of help?"

"I'm selling tomatoes," he said. "I thought perhaps you'd be interested in buying this basket full."

It was only then that I noticed the basket in his hands, as though suddenly illuminated by the offer, precariously but evenly balanced in both hands like a treasure. I looked harder as he seemed to come clearer under the dusky opaqueness of moonrise. I noticed his hair was a lush brush of unspotted white (as if a thousand years had woven webs of whiteness on his head). His upper torso was wrapped in a thick woolen coat, one of which I'd not seen in these parts in the last decade, at least. His chin, wet with sweat, rested on a scarf thrown carelessly around his neck and tucked into the opening of his coat in the front. A boutonniere protruded from a lapel. His trousers of bright purple seemed to pierce my recessing eyes. Even though they were partly covered with garden dirt, the red shoes adorning his feet glistened in the night's dimness.

After I recovered from his impressive appearance I managed to say, "Thanks, but I have my own tomato garden." I recalled the efforts my wife, daughters, I and, before he died, Anan, had put into the garden.

I made to return to my family, but he hastened a response. I was glad he did, as I didn't want to leave him yet. "These are special tomatoes," he said.

"Special tomatoes? How so?"

My famished curiosity must have been palpable, for he fed it well: "They are redder and richer and sweeter. You've never had any like these. I guarantee you that. Why don't you try one?"

His claim sounded false on its face, even outrageous. Tomatoes are tomatoes. How different could one be from the other? But how could I say that? Recollecting Anan's exceptional pride and effort in tomato gardening, it had to stand to reason that exceptional effort could produce special tomatoes. Teased by this false logic, I had to believe him. Nor was it simply what he said that prompted pause. It was also the manner he said it, the confidence he put in his words that was so daunting, and the way he held himself within the dawning night. Holding a tomato in a hand pushed toward me, he said,

Here, try one."

Could they truly be sweeter? There was only one way to find out. I grabbed the tomato and took a bite. As I chewed on it his face lit with the recognition of I told you so. And at first I wasn't sure, but then his tomato tasted sweeter, perhaps a lot sweeter than any I'd ever had. "I told you these are special tomatoes," he reminded me. "Won't you buy this basket full?"

"I will," said I. "But you, who are you?"

"I'm a trader of sorts."

"I wonder… I've never seen you before. Your name?"

"Call me Nana," he said.

"Well, Nana, you have made yourself a new customer."

And with that I bought the basket of tomatoes over a handshake. I realized he had garden dirt on his hands that transferred to mine after we shook.

I took the tomatoes indoors to my wife and daughters, announcing the purchase and uniqueness of the tomatoes with vigor. My wife Eno looked them over, rolled her eyes and stifled what I suspected was a strained laughter laced with mockery. That annoyed me. "Try some for yourself and you'll see," I challenged her. "You too, Abena and Ama," I instructed my daughters. My wife refused, but my children obeyed.

"Well?" I asked.

Said Ama, "I've never tasted tomatoes this good."

"And you, Abena, what do you think?"

"They taste very sweet, Papa," she said. "As sweet as sugar."

"Idiot!" I screamed. "How can tomatoes taste like sugar?"

We ate the rest of supper in silence, my anger corrupting the air like bad fecal stench. After the meal, Eno asked Ama to take the tomatoes to the kitchen, saying, "We'll make a tomato meal tomorrow. Since they are so sweet perhaps they will taste like a meal of sugar."

A meal of sugar. I suspected she'd said that to irritate me. (Could Anan's death be making her so irritable?) And irritated I was as I went and sat outside. Why couldn't she see the wisdom of my decision? She was simply ignorant, I concluded.

The next day I summoned the entire family to go to the garden to harvest our tomatoes. I'd show them how inferior ours were to Nana's. But there were no tomatoes to be harvested. "How could this have happened?" I wondered aloud.

"Someone has stolen our tomatoes," Abena cried.

I was angry with her. Need she state the obvious? But now I saw an opportunity to turn this misfortune to my advantage. "You see how much foresight I have?" I asked. "If I hadn't bought those tomatoes yesterday, we'd have no tomatoes to eat today."

We went back to work growing more tomatoes. And how I wished Anan was there to help us. Working on the garden seemed to help us, though. Even under the sun's spanking, we would each recall something about Anan – the way he held a hoe over the soil, how he wiped a wayward sweat from his eyes, his face-wide grin – all observed when he'd joined us to work the little garden of tomatoes.

As it were, Nana's tomatoes served us well for a long time and the rest of the family partook of them without dissent. And while it lasted it seemed the family had found peace post-Anan. Most days, the family would gather near the garden and recollect Anan's folktales. We were anticipating the next harvest. Had I restored the status quo ante?

Some time later, the day before harvest, Nana returned. This time he was a wobbling mass of flesh – a sow approaching with leisurely pace, short and almost one with the soil as a snake. And his hair was now darker than bitumen. Despite this changed appearance, I knew it was

Nana. Again he carried a basket of tomatoes. His voice was mellow, but he didn't have to convince me this time. I bought the basket of tomatoes and invited Nana to join the family for supper. He declined. "For our mutual good," he explained.

When I took the tomatoes indoors, this time Eno refused to sheath her disappointment. "These tomatoes are the same as any..."

"Be quiet!" I stormed out of the room, utterly infuriated. I refused to partake in the family supper, preferring instead to feast on a couple of Nana's tomatoes, relishing every taste of their fleshy redness. It surprised me that Eno behaved as such. Didn't she realize what was at stake? Had she forgotten what peace Nana's tomatoes had brought us the last time?

The next day, I summoned the family to go to our garden to harvest tomatoes. But, again, all the tomatoes were gone. "Someone has stolen our tomatoes," Ama wailed.

"Be quiet!" I yelled. "Now you see how wise I was buying Nana's tomatoes!"

Once more, we had to rely on Nana's tomatoes for a long time as we started growing our own again. And peace was restored as before.

The next time Nana came was the night before harvest. I was waiting for him – as though I expected him. It was as if a spiritual bond had grown between us. This time he was of medium height, his head was bald like calabash and he wore a goatee.

"Nana," I said before he could speak. "I have missed you. Here, give me those tomatoes."

He smiled and asked, "I will be seeing you?" And then he was gone, faster than the darkening horizon that swallowed him. I wanted to chase after him, beg him to help me. How could I face the family solo? How could I close the abiding chasm Anan's death had caused?

My family greeted me with silence when I took the tomatoes indoors. But because none voiced disappointment, I had to bury the abuse I'd practiced in case anyone said anything unkind about Nana's tomatoes. I supposed they'd either seen the wisdom of my ways or surrendered to my will.

The next morning we faced an empty tomato garden. Again. "You see," I told my wife Eno. "Once again I have saved us from tomato drought."

Slowly, ever so slowly, she turned to me and said, "My dear, have you wondered how every time Nana brings his tomatoes we come to an empty tomato garden?"

"What are you saying?" I asked.

She didn't respond.

Later that night, there was too much tension in the house, too much left unspoken. Had I worsened matters with Nana's tomatoes? I pretended to excuse myself, telling my family I was going to visit my friend Ananse. But instead, unobtrusively like a spider, I hid in a corner of the room beyond Suspicion's reach.

After some idle talk, I heard Ama ask, "What do you think of these tomatoes?"

"Has anyone ever seen this Nana that Papa says has been selling him tomatoes?" asked Abena.

Perceptive. Very perceptive, Abena.

"No. Have you?"

"No."

"None of you have seen him?" Eno asked. "How come?"

"Remember we are indoors whenever he comes," said Ama. "Papa goes outside for a while and comes back with a basket of tomatoes."

"Have you noticed that whenever Papa brings the tomatoes he seems out of breadth and his feet are dirty?" asked Abena.

Oh, Abena, where are you going with this?

"Where does that leave us?" asked Ama.

"The elders have a saying," Eno remarked. "It is the fool whose own tomatoes are sold to him. But I don't believe your Papa is a fool."

Or am I? Anan, am I a fool? Nana, am I a fool?

That got me wondering, not so much over my folly (or lack of it), but over he (or they) who had prompted Eno's remark. I wondered if I'd ever see him again. If I saw him again, will it be in the summons of my wishes? A time of joy and celebration? Will we dance like brothers under sunrays? Would I successfully and permanently have communicated the joy of his tomatoes to my wife and daughters the way he communicated it to me? Or will I see him in hidden corridors of despair because of the inadequacy of doppelgangers? Will we remain hidden under moon clouds? Will I be waiting at my doorstep coughing, spitting, crying, sweating, defecating, urinating, farting, bleeding, sneezing, puking? Shall I be in fear of shadows creeping into the closets of the home? Or shall I be in a calm state of welcome? If I saw Nana again, would I be a fool whose own tomatoes are sold to him? Fool? But … I am not a fool.

Or am I?

CHAPTER TWO

***

Embrace of the Shadows

You can do it! You can do it! You can do it! The rending chants chorused the long pauses in my distressed breath. The frenzied voices gave me cover, like blankets for additional warmth—so many human beings could not be wrong. My body responded with profuse perspiration as though each pore was weeping a heaving tear, one after another. As I held the machete in my hand and closed my eyes, Mojo's summons returned to me: *This is the test of your loyalty to us. Do not fail*!

But as the bound prisoner lay in front of me on the grassless ground and as the men in the camp chanted me on, I just couldn't bring myself to slit his throat as Mojo had directed or, if I preferred, stab his chest in the left part and draw his lifeblood over my body.

Before we can fully accept you, you have to be able to do this.

And God knows I needed acceptance. Where else could I turn? To whom? Only yesterday, Pa and Ma were with me. But since the bomb fell, not only was I was rendered homeless but also parentless. And to think that this had been a war that neither of them wanted.

Pa was a well-paid clerk in the local branch of the Ministry of Finance and Ma an administrative assistant in the Ministry of Tourism, although I often heard her say that there was little to do as tourists had stopped coming ever since our country's leader was accused of masterminding an attack on an airplane flying from America to the UK. "We are now a pariah state," Pa once said at dinner, at a time when I thought I heard someone at the door. But when I opened the door to check, there was no one there. And we never discussed the matter after that until I brought it up sometime later by asking Pa why so many people in the world hated our country. "Who told you that?" he asked.

22

I could have told him that his own words about our country becoming a pariah sufficed, but he had probably said it in a moment of carelessness and quickly forgotten it. "Some of my school friends told me," I said. "They complained that our Great Leader is reckless and has gotten us into trouble."

I wasn't sure, but I thought I saw a flash of fear in Pa's eyes when he told me, "Don't ever listen to such nonsense and don't ever take part in such talk. Do you hear me?"

I nodded, but he must not have been convinced because he held me firmly by both elbows and said sternly, "Listen very carefully. Both your mother and I are civil servants. Do you know what that means? The government is our employer. It is the government that pays us and it is with that pay that we feed and clothe you and send you to school and pay the rent for our apartment. Don't ever be caught saying or even listening to any bad talk about the government or our Great Leader."

"Okay, Pa."

He must still not have been convinced, as this time he held me by the ears. "Do you know what happens to people who say bad things about the government?"

He didn't have to tell me. I had heard of the numerous accounts of arrests and killings in the jailhouses of both real and perceived enemies of the government. In fact, a few people had disappeared from our apartment, rumored to have been abducted at night by government agents. Little was said about them, except in hushed voices—heard by eavesdroppers—suggesting that the abductees were engaged in subversive activities. So I could appreciate Pa's concern, especially given that he wouldn't want to do anything to disturb our relative comfort. We lived in a fairly good neighborhood, mostly populated by government employees, with our rents heavily subsidized by the government. Ma even told me that our groceries were affordable because the government subsidized those as well. She said the government even subsidized my school fees.

Based on Pa's reaction, I regretted telling him about what I'd heard in school. After all, this wasn't the first time I'd heard bad things about the government. Apart from the abductions, imprisoning and killing of those the government took to be its enemies, I heard stories of all kinds of corruptions in high places—from the looting of national coffers to carnal immorality, some of which involved the coercion of citizens to sacrifice themselves or their daughters for the somatic pleasures of our country's leaders.

Perhaps Pa could see the fear his actions were causing me. He removed his hands from my ears, relaxed a little and said, "I didn't mean to upset you, but this is no idle matter."

"I understand, Pa," I said to forestall experiencing any other form of physical distress he might impose.

I would not have given his warnings much thought until some time later when I heard at school that a group of citizens had organized a militia and was beginning to fight government forces in certain towns, demanding the dismantling of the current government, including the immediate resignation of our Great Leader.

I thought things were working out well for us and couldn't appreciate why anyone would make such a demand. At fifteen, I was doing well in school and hoped to study business at the national university. My family and I lived a decent, if not wealthy life, and no one really bothered us. We had three good meals a day, had a television set that broadcast many hours of our Great Leader's accomplishments, felt safe in the streets and could even roam them at night without fear of muggers and other scofflaws. We also were left to worship God, however we perceived Him. Why would anyone want to change this? So, yes, there were those stories of the jailing and killing and whatnot, but why get on the bad side of the government to begin with? To me, it seemed you just kept quiet about the government and went about your affairs and you were okay. If the government made any demands on you, you just cooperated. Simple as that. And if others hated our country, I didn't like it, but that was their problem.

But now some people had to make trouble by forming a militia. I expected that the government would fight back and defeat the wayward militia in no time. Our

Great Leader went on national television to say so, and I believed him. But months after he made his speech, the fighting continued. One day we would hear that the rebels had taken a town here and the next day we would hear that the government had retaken it and then later the rebels would take it back. The seesawing of political and military muscling continued for several months and no one could tell which side would prevail.

As these events unfolded, Pa became unusually quiet and even the more gregarious Ma spoke less. In fact, their somberness seemed to affect just about everybody I knew, even more so when we heard that NATO had begun to drop bombs on government forces after accusing the government of human rights abuses.

"They hate us," Ma said one night. "They have just found an excuse to get rid of the government." And then after a pause, she added, "But I wish the government would just leave."

"So we can have some peace," Pa added. "I don't like what the rebels have started, but right now I don't care who is wrong or right; I just want this shadow over our heads to go away." Pa looked at me, staring into my eyes. I could see the fear hinted in his eyes as he said to me, "You never heard us say what we just said." This time he made no physical contact to ensure that I would comply. Perhaps he was just weary.

Pa walked into the sultry night to clear his head.

The next day we saw government forces in our town for the first time. We could see their armored cars on the streets and we knew that the fight had now been brought to us. "The government forces are here in retreat," I heard in school. "The rebels are winning in the other cities and the government has to pull away. They are trying to regroup and launch a counter attack."

I knew that unless the government forces moved out of our town, the rebels were likely to come after them. I was afraid, but Ma assured me that all would be well. The government would protect us and the rebels couldn't do any harm.

She didn't sound convincing.

We were in school when we heard the sound of aircrafts, soon followed by indescribably loud sounds—deafening as if a million guns were being fired at once. In the ensuing pandemonium as everyone, including adults ran, I too ran toward the place where I expected the greatest comfort.

But home no longer existed.

I could barely believe the rubble that it had been reduced to. Panting as my breath came in short spurts from exhaustion, I panicked. Where were Ma and Pa? It was a little after noon—just the time when Ma and Pa came home for lunch and a short siesta before returning to work for the afternoon shift. All around, commotion mounted as people ran here and there, shrieking and yelling, uttering all manner of groans.

As I stood there staring at the rubble, fear and worry increasingly wrenching me, one of the elders in the apartment—I put him around sixty—approached me, his face stained with blood, a new limp in his left leg, that also oozed blood.

"Sorry, son," he said. "Your parents were both in there when the bomb dropped."

"No!"

"I saw them enter the building with my own two eyes. I was standing over there."

He pointed to a part of the road a little farther down. "I was coming back from one of my afternoon walks when I saw them enter—first your mother and then your father. And then in a split second there was a plane flying over and then a deafening sound and then this... I was thrown several feet into the air. It's a miracle I survived."

"That can't be," I said.

"Why would I lie?"

"My father and mother are alive. They're not in there."

"I know this is hard for you. It is hard for me too. But I think God saved me for a purpose. I will take care of you."

"My parents are alive!"

He was a liar!

Before he could respond, a truck pulled up to us.

"What are you doing?" A shades-wearing man pulled out his neck and asked us.

"I live there," the elderly man said, pointing to what used to be home. "They have killed his parents. Both his father and mother are buried in there."

"That building must have been ... no, that building was harboring government informants and forces," the man in shades said.

"There were no government forces or informants in there," the elderly neighbor said.

"Are you contradicting me?" the shaded man asked. He made a quick movement of his head—which I realized was a signal—and the man seated next to him yelped orders and in one instant we were being manhandled and tossed into the back of the truck, where, as the vehicle began to move forward, we were gagged and bound by hands and feet. Before the gagging, I yelled several times and received well-constructed kicks to my belly region. I counted eight men in the back of the truck, all of them shirtless, all of them toting rifles. I felt something akin to hopelessness that is very hard to describe, as if the world had ended. A numbness laced with anger. Because this feeling was so overwhelmingly disempowering, perhaps what I felt was in essence nothing but a numbing despondent state of being.

The truck moved at varying speeds, turning corners so fast it sometimes seemed it would overturn. The sound of gunfire became an irritating soundtrack with its *ra ta ta ta ta* chorus, so continual it quickly became familiar and acquired a rhythmic, perversely soothing effect. "We are headed to base," I heard one of the captors declare. "Looks like it's too dangerous to stay around town." At the time when I heard this, I tried to move, intending to signal to my captors that I didn't concur with going out of town. My reward was a blow to the solar plexus, which turned my world into a void.

When I overcame the unconsciousness and opened my eyes, the first thing I noticed was the darkening sky and the realization that I was lying on my back in the open. I concluded that twilight was fast approaching—the sky was sunless, holding an expanse of fading blue. I recalled Ma and Pa and blinked hard to forestall the falling of tears. I couldn't stay in the state for long, though, as I heard the words, "He is finally waking up." When I looked around, I realized that tents had been pitched in the short distances all around the opening where I lay, beyond which there were only trees and grass. I moved my hands and legs to try and wake them up and took solace in the knowledge that I was unbound and that the gag had been removed.

The previously shaded man walked over to me (but this time he wasn't wearing his sunglasses.) His hands by his sides, he stood over me, staring directly for a long while into my eyes as if he wanted to steal my spirit. "My name is Mojo," he said. "Welcome to the Boys of Company M, a battalion of the MOJO." I said nothing, my thoughts as rudderless as wind. Mojo moved his hands from the sides to the front, bringing into focus the machete in his hand.

"From now on your name shall be Jomo," he said.

"My name is…"

He brought the machete down hard, plunging it into the earth inches from my face. I flinched as he retrieved it and declared, "You have no other name than Jomo. If I hear you call yourself by any other name, you shall surely die." Mojo paused, as though he wanted to give me time to assimilate his warning, while he brandished the machete, holding it delicately to his chest from time to time as if he considered it a treasure. "So, now, tell me, what is your name?"

He held the machete over my head.

"Jomo," I said.

"I can't hear you."

"Jomo!"

"Louder"

"Jomo!!!" My belly ached from this forced outburst.

"Good," Mojo said.

By now, a crowd had gathered around us, some still sporting shades. If ever the word motley was appropriate, it would well describe the people I saw around me: young and old, fat and thin, muscular and flabby, mostly bare-chested men, whose shorts and trousers span all colors of the rainbow and beyond, some of them so bright you would think they were modeling for some clothing boutique with a bizarre sense of color.

"We will initiate you tonight," Mojo said. "Ojom," he called. One of the tallest men present came forward in response. "Get Omoj to help you prepare Jomo for initiation."

Ojom left and soon returned with a squat man that I surmised to be Omoj. They helped me to my feet and led me outside the tents into the bushes.

"Strip!" Ojom ordered.

I didn't respond. Omoj broke a thin branch from a tree behind him and snapped it in two. He kept one part of the branch and gave the other to Ojom. Next I knew, Ojom had tripped me. I felt the sting of the branch on my back before I hit the ground, and another. I cried out despite my resolve to play macho. I writhed on the ground as they continued with the lashing. Once, I tried to get up and ran, but a hand grabbed me and brought me back down. After about eight more lashes, they stopped.

35

Ojom brought his face close to mine. Even before he spoke, his foul breath irritated my nostrils. "When we ask you to do something, you do it! No hesitation, no questions. Kapish?"

If only to escape the assault of unwashed mouth, liquor and smell of rotten meat, I responded, "Yes."

"Good," Ojom said. "Now strip."

As embarrassed as I was, I had no desire to experience more lashes and foul breaths. I removed my shirt and trousers. "Strip naked is what I meant," Ojom informed me. I removed my underwear.

Ojom and Omoj pointed toward my groin area and started laughing. "But you are a boy yet," said Omoj. "By the time we are through with you, you would have become a man. And you will be bigger there too." They continued to laugh for at least a minute.

"Go get his uniform," Ojom instructed Omoj who left and returned with pair of shorts.

Ojom asked that I put them on. The loose shorts, which smelled of urine, reached down to my knees and were held at the waist by a string that I had to tie into a knot.

"You look like a model," Omoj said. "Now let's take you back to Mojo."

Mojo was seated on a tree stump in his tent when I was brought to his presence. The tent was lit by a number of lanterns. There were various objects on the ground around him and behind him on opposite sides were two wooden boxes.

"I see you are settling down," Mojo said. "Let me welcome you to our camp. Pardon me for my rudeness before..."

A man entered the tent to announce, "We have prepared the sacrifice, sir."

"Thank you Omoj Number Two, we shall be out soon." Omoj Number Two Left. "As I was saying," Mojo continued, "welcome. You should have guessed by now that everyone here bears a variation of the name Mojo. I, as leader, carry that name for myself. That is one way we create common identity. We need everyone to lose their prior identity and instead identify with MOJO, which is an acronym for Movement of Justice and Openness."

He smiled. "Our cause is noble in that we intend to restore justice to our dear country, which has been hijacked for too long by thieves and demagogues and hooligans and murderers. From what your neighbor tells me, you have lost your parents. But don't worry; we will give you a new family. Yes, we will help you mourn your mother and father, but you will soon find that your pain will be numbed by the family we will give you. But every family has rituals, things that bind it together. So we want you to join us, but before you do so, there is one task that you must accomplish. Before we can fully accept you, you have to be able to do this. "

Emboldened by his ongoing smile, I said, 'Sir, I want to go home."

His smile disappeared, as if into the frown that replaced it. "What did you say?"

I was more hesitant this time, but I repeated my request to go home.

He asked me to come closer to him. "You no longer have a home but this one," he said. "Strip!" Remembering what happened at the hands of Omoj and Ojom, I complied immediately. "I hate to do this, but I must. We value order and discipline in this camp." He picked a long stick from the ground and asked me to bend over and touch my toes. He began to hit after I did so. At the second hit, I yelled and moved my hands to soothe my backside. "I am giving you six strokes, but anytime you touch your buttocks, I will start from count one." That said, he started recounting from one. I was crying at the fourth strike, six if you include the two he'd discounted, and had an indescribable yearning to soothe my buttocks, but knew I had to bear it until he was finished or have him start afresh. When he was finished, he asked me to put on my shorts.

"You have to be tough, Jomo. It is necessary for survival. No more crying."

Still in pain from my sore backside, but afraid that I would endure more lashing if I didn't obey, I endeavored to bring the crying under control, forcing it into sniffles and then deep breaths.

"Good," Mojo said. He took a machete from the ground and shoved it into my hand. "We have determined that the old man who was with you this afternoon was a government informant. He needs to die. And we have decided to give you the honor of performing the killing. As we speak, everyone has gathered outside and the old man is in the center of the circle they've formed. Your task is to kill him. It's your choice—either slit his throat or stab him in the chest on this side where his heart is." He pointed to his left chest. "This is the test of your loyalty to us. Do not fail!"

I wanted to tell him that it was too early for him to expect any loyalty and that I couldn't do the killing anyway, but I was afraid of what he might do to me. I wanted to tell him also that the so called government informant was a good man. He always had a kind word to say whenever I saw him in the apartment or neighborhood. He had even bought me a soccer ball once. And he bought us Christmas gifts. And a number of times, when I was

40

younger, Pa and Ma had left me with him for hours at his insistence when they went out on a special date.

Dumbfounded, I could barely respond when Mojo took my free hand and led me outside into the center of the circle. I wanted to reflect, to mourn my parents if indeed they were dead, give them the due tribute of a pained heart. But matters were moving too fast for me to even do this. Instead, I looked at the man as the crowd of no less than a hundred urged me on with chants and gestures. I moved to the man but my body shook so badly I could barely stand still. He looked at me, fear palpably in his eyes even under the relative dimness of moonlight.

I don't know how long I stood there shaking before Mojo came and grabbed me by the hand and led me back into his tent. He was accompanied by three others. This time, they did the stripping, held me down and lashed me for minutes, oblivious to my protesting yells of pain. When they were done, Mojo went to the wooded box in the right corner of the room and retrieved a bottle. "This is my makeshift bodega," he said. He took a swig from the bottle and gave it to me. "Drink," he ordered, "and don't stop until I tell you to."

The brown firewater burned my throat and insides, but I forced myself to swallow and swallow and swallow, until Mojo asked me to stop. He took the bottle from me. In minutes I felt a new level of strength. "We will try this again," Mojo said. "The man outside there is an evil man. He has informed on many families, caused them to be arrested and killed. This is necessary revolutionary justice. He must die. Again, let me say it. This is the test of your loyalty to us. Do not fail!"

He led me outside again, with the machete in my hand. I sweated as the almost anonymous crowd chanted and gestured me on for the kill. I moved with more determination without the previous body-shaking. I was becoming fear's more terrible twin, conquering it. But as I stood next to the man, I remembered his face in earlier times, the kind grin, his charm even when he'd not shaved and stubbles of white dotted his chin, the dimple on his thin face, the depth of joy in his eyes anytime he greeted me. I couldn't do it.

Jomo and three others took me back inside the tent. My backside was so sore from the earlier beatings that despite my state of relative intoxication, I cried when they lashed my bare backside once again. After this was done and Mojo had ordered me to stop crying, he brought from the box on the right side of the tent leaves that I suspected to be marijuana. I had seen pictures of the leaves in magazines but never the real thing. Mojo rolled some up into a joint in an old newspaper and lit it. He asked me to smoke.

When he led me outside again, I was in different state of mind that is hard to describe, calmed and unafraid, believing I could do anything. I approached with resolve to accomplish the task, but once again I remembered the elderly man walking down the street wishing God's blessings on everyone he met and receiving blessings in equal measure. I remembered him attending to a dog on the side of the street that had just been struck by a car.

"This is your last chance!" Mojo warned this time after I had been beaten once more following my most recent failure. The blood from my backside informed me that my body couldn't take much more of this punishment.

Again from that box in the right corner of the room, Mojo brought out some powdery substance and, from the box on the right, a number of pictures. He pointed to a man in one of the pictures with a grandfatherly face filled up with a grin. "He had three daughters when the government arrested him for so called subversive activities. He never returned home." He showed me ten pictures, each with a story, depicting families torn apart, great promise and aspirations smashed. And then the next group of ten pictures was of dead bodies, some mutilated, some bearing gunshots, others dismembered. "This is what the information he fed the government led to. We have been observing him for a long time, so don't think this is arbitrary. We know what he's been doing. Why do you think of all the people in the street we stopped by him? You... Let's just say that you were a collateral catch. And, seeing your distress when he said your parents had perished, I felt some responsibility for you. After all, the bomb was dropped in support of our campaign to unseat the government. I regret that your parents died, but in such times innocent lives sadly perish. When all this is over, we will honor them, but now to the matter at hand, as you can see, that monster deserves to die."

My body was weak; I could barely think on account of what had been done to it so far. Mojo now poured part of the powdery substance onto the back of his palm and asked me to sniff it. I did.

I was invincible.

I was invisible.

Outside, the world was transformed. I could hear chants that had the force of a symphony, grand gestures with operatic energy. Each face belonged to an angel. The Milky Way had opened up a pathway into the heavens that I could travel to accomplish the divinely entrusted task of ending the evil before me. I walked forward with purpose. My heart beat not with fear but with the anticipation of accomplishment. I looked down at the beast in front of me, horns protruding from its head, its canine teeth as long as cleavers, eyes red as blood. This hideousness was an affront to humanity. The crowd's music continued to play and its performance increased in tempo, urging me on. I stood emboldened, strong as Samson, except this would not be my last but first strength. I raised the machete and brought it down into the flesh of the beast. As the crescendo of the music signaled approval, I felt the warm bath of the beast's blood on my hand. I raised the machete one more time and brought it down into the reluctant embrace of the beast.

CHAPTER THREE

***

The Interview

As Latif approached the brick-walled building, he focused on its sole doorknob. But distracted when a man walked out of the building displaying a furrowed brow and a tight frown, Latif wondered what could cause such facial distress. "Don't go in there," the man said, scampering away before Latif could recover from the weighty words.

Don't go in there? No; that wasn't what the man said, Latif contradicted his own ears. The man had said rather, "Do go in there." That was the only entreaty worthy of consideration, Latif said to himself. How could anyone hinder his progress when he was so close? That fleeting self-debate settled, Latif moved even more determinedly toward the building, imagining its plush, air conditioned offices.

47

He had been walking for at least thirty minutes. The high humidity that filled the air combined with the burning sun to tease copious amounts of perspiration from his body. As he hurried forward and wiped the relentless sweat from his face with a soaked handkerchief, he regretted not having taken a bus. Was this sweat-bath worth the few dollars he'd saved by walking?

When he reached the building, he paused to tighten his tie, loosened earlier for comfort, and to put on the jacket of the suit he'd borrowed from Isaiah. At that moment, he wished the building had one of those sliding glass doors that allowed for self-reflection so that he could make sure his appearance passed the mark. Also, he could have derived assurance from the familiarity of his features—the broad headed, clean shaven, chin-dimpled face—that Akos had repeatedly told him were the most charming she'd ever seen. But no, he confronted the brick wall, a tiny door in the middle, and firmly shuttered windows. So the *façade* wasn't what he expected, but he had to look beyond that.

Latif settled for one more thorough wipe of facial sweat. With a deep breath he touched the doorknob. It wouldn't turn. He tried turning it a second time to no avail. He pushed the door. It was firmly closed. He turned the knob one more time. When he obtained no success, he stepped back to examine the knob optically.

It was at that time that the door opened. Even from the outside, he could feel the reach of the building's air conditioned air. But for the woman standing in the doorway, Latif would have leapt forward into the building. "May I help you?" the woman asked, tossing her head one way to throw back long hair that seemed stranded on her pale face.

Latif stepped forward. "Yes, madam," he said. "I am Isaiah Johnson. I have an interview with Mr. Doherty."

The woman frowned. "Isaiah Johnson?"

"Yes, madam, that's me." Latif smiled, but the woman's frown remained.

"Are you sure you're Isaiah Johnson?"

"Yes, madam, I am."

"Can I see a picture ID? I didn't expect an Isaiah Johnson to look like you."

Latif produced the State ID that Isaiah Johnson had given him. "Just in case," Isaiah had said with prescience. "You can use my papers till you get yours. Don't worry, they can't tell the difference between us. But be prepared—they're usually surprised to find out that my name is Isaiah Johnson. Born and bred in Ghana and they wonder how I can bear that name."

The woman interchangeably studied the ID and Latif's face for almost a minute.

Madam, it's burning outside here; can I please come in and get the full enjoyment of your air conditioned air? This question only hovered in Latif's mind and remained unasked for fear of causing offense.

"Well, I guess you're right. You are Isaiah Johnson. Come in."

The woman stepped back, making room for Latif to enter the building, by which time he was again still with sweat, and he could feel the wetness run down his back and thighs. "My name is Anna Doherty," the woman said, extending a hand. As Latif shook it, she added, "Welcome to our offices."

"Thank you, madam."

"You can call me Mrs. Doherty," she said. "Please have a seat while I tell Mr. Doherty you're here."

Latif's first instinct was to remove his handkerchief, but he realized that the conditioned air had dried his face already. He looked around the reception area. Replica paintings of Picasso and Van Gogh adorned the walls and a few magazines were sprawled on a table in front of three cushioned chairs. Latif sat on one of the chairs while Mrs. Doherty did likewise behind the receptionist's desk in front of the chairs and table. She dialed a number. "Mr. Johnson is here for his interview," she said. After she hung up she informed Latif, "Mr. Doherty is tied up for a few minutes. He will see you as soon as he can."

"Thanks," Latif said. Unable to find a subject to introduce, he picked up a magazine lying on the table, but he couldn't concentrate on reading.

The phone in the reception area rang and Mrs. Doherty picked it up. "The consignment?" she said. "Okay, you mean the delivery. I will tell him. Into the bank account? Okay, that shouldn't be a problem." Mrs. Doherty shook her head as she hung up the phone.

What kind of firm handled consignments and deliveries? Latif wondered but said nothing. After about ten minutes of silence, he decided to engage Mrs. Doherty. Perhaps she could offer him some tips for the interview. "It's very quiet here, just the kind of environment I like working in," he said.

"Yes," Mrs. Doherty replied.

Yes what? Latif wondered. "Is it always like this?"

"Yes."

Perhaps he needed a new topic to tease out her words. "You know, Mrs. Doherty," Latif said, "I was just wondering. How did you know I was outside? Did you hear me trying to turn the doorknob?

"No, I didn't hear you turn the knob. We have surveillance cameras outside that monitor what goes on. You probably didn't see them because they're hidden in the corners. You have to really look to notice them. But they work very well. We have only had two attacks since we installed them last month."

"Attacks? What kinds of attacks?"

"Well, roughly two weeks ago our clerk was shot as he was entering the building, but thanks to our cameras the police were able to catch the assailants."

"What happened to the victim?

"He died on the spot."

"And the attack before that?"

"That was against his predecessor. The assailant followed a client into the building. We thought he was with the client. Anyhow, once he got into the building he entered Tim's office, that's the first one you see after this reception room. I wasn't here at the time. He stabbed Tim to death, but the partners managed to overcome him before he could cause further harm."

"And the nature of the other attacks before that?"

"Identical. Mostly gunshots and stabbings."

Why was she telling him all this? Was it a manner of foretelling in order to forearm?

Latif realized that the artificially conditioned air had gotten much colder. He tightened his tie and what had seemed a slight hum of the air conditioning system now became an intrusive drone, as annoying as the buzz of mosquitoes that used to plague his night's sleep back home. "So... so... if I am hired," he said, "which one will be my office?"

"The first one after this reception room. We have only one office for the clerk and that's the one that you'll have."

Latif breathed in deeply as he recalled the contents of the newspaper advertisement. His memory detailed it clearly: Doherty Rodgers Upchurch Gross & Sorensen/Clerk needed/No experience necessary/Will train. This was followed by the address and phone number. Isaiah had shown him the advertisement, encouraging him to apply. "Man, it doesn't get better than this. Can you imagine that a law firm doesn't need any experience? I know you have a law degree and this is just for a clerk's position but, given how things are going, you could use this as a start. It has to be better than nothing."

Isaiah was right. Since arriving in the US on a visitor's visa a month ago, Latif had interviewed with over twenty firms. None had hired him. Isaiah had allowed him to stay gratis in his Rogers Park studio apartment and shown Latif some of the tourist attractions of Chicago, including the serenely verdant Grant Park, the amusements of Navy Pier overlooking Lake Michigan, and the colossus that was Willis Tower. And they would sometimes sit at home and drink cheap whiskey and reminisce over family and friends in Ghana. But how long could Latif live on drinks, reminisces, hope and the attractions of the Windy City? He needed to find a job before his two month visa expired, and then he would move out of Latif's studio, get established and begin to work on obtaining a green card. He would probably have to marry an American woman for that. Of course, because of Akos Johnson, it would have to be a marriage of convenience.

He remembered the last conversation he'd had with Akos. "You have to promise you'll come back and marry me," she'd said.

"How can you doubt that, Akos? After five years, how can I even look at another woman?"

"That's what they all say. Even though they were married, Freema's husband divorced her after only one year there."

Latif had decided that deeds, not words, would demonstrate his commitment and fidelity. He would regularize his stay as soon as possible, raise sufficient funds, and give Akos a befitting marriage, comprising both a traditional ceremony with loads of gifts for her family and a grand wedding with an impressive banquet to follow. She deserved this not merely because he loved her but because she had sacrificed so much for him. When after he graduated with a law degree from the University of Ghana he could find no employment, she was the one who provided him pocket money, consoled him whenever his father called him a "useless lawyer who still lives with his parents." A meal or a word of encouragement was ample, if brief, balm for the bleeding emotional wounds. As a nurse, she only earned enough for one and yet she'd always share her earnings with him. He had suggested moving into her apartment, but she wouldn't allow that. "Not until we're married," she'd say.

Unemployed, he would saunter the streets of Accra by day and ask for work, the vicious sun squeezing copious amounts of sweat from his body. Invariably rejected, he'd join a growing number of his compatriots in street corners to watch in envy the closed, obviously well air-conditioned, chauffeured Benzs and Jaguars drive by. Sometimes, they'd walk to the marketplace to plead for food as blind songsmiths scrounged for alms with ballads under the gaze of vultures hovering over rubbish damps. By night, when Akos wasn't working late, he'd be with her in moonlit corners and she'd listen to his expressions of love as well as his laments, particularly his wish to find better prospects elsewhere. "I hate this situation," he'd say. "I hate the Accra heat and I hate my poverty. I wish I could fly to a cooler place with job opportunities, a place like America. But I have no wings." On some days, he cried as he said this.

She would rather have him with her, Akos said, but she couldn't stand to see him so broken. So it was Akos who had her cousin Isaiah Johnson, a taxi driver in Chicago, send him an invitation letter and a bank statement, which he had used to obtain the visitor's visa to Chicago. Isaiah had himself left an analyst's job with the Ghana Ministry of Finance in Accra some three years before and ended up driving a taxi in Chicago after fruitless job searches. When Akos pointed this out, Latif replied, "I have a law degree. I hear Americans like to sue. They will need my services."

And so it was Akos who borrowed money from her uncle to buy the plane ticket from Accra. It was Akos…

"Mr. Doherty will see you now," Mrs. Doherty announced. "His office is the third on the right."

"Thank you," Latif said, as he stood up and walked in the indicated direction.

On his way to Mr. Doherty's office, he heard voices coming from the other partners' closed offices. He knocked when he got to the door that bore Richard Doherty's name. A booming voice invited him in. He entered the office and immediately closed his eyes. There seemed to be lights everywhere and the office was one massive space of disturbing incandescence.

"Oh!" Richard Doherty exclaimed. "The light must be bothering you. Don't worry, you will get used to it. Come in and have a seat."

Now squinting, Latif struggled to walk through the lights to find the chair in front of Mr. Doherty's desk. He was able to determine that there were multiple illuminants on the desk, walls and from the ceiling. Those behind Mr. Doherty shone directly at him, hurting his eyes, making it difficult for him to pick out the exact details of Mr. Doherty's face or frame. He could tell, though, that the man was massive, towering above the desk.

"So what can I do for you?" Mr. Doherty asked.

"I am here for our interview," Latif said.

"Yes, that's right, you answered our ad. But why should I hire you?"

"Sir, I am dedicated and intelligent and…"

"And you are Isaiah Johnson?"

"Yes, sir."

"You don't sound like an Isaiah Johnson. Is that your real name?"

"Yes, sir."

"But that accent, where is it from?"

"I was born in Ghana."

"Africa, right?"

"Yes, sir."

"So you changed your name, picked up an American name when you got here."

"No, sir. I was born Isaiah Johnson."

"But what kind of an African name is Isaiah Johnson?"

"My first name is from the Bible. I was named after Isaiah the prophet. The second name is the family name."

"Johnson?"

"Yes, sir. We had a lot of contact with Europeans. The name was probably adopted by my ancestors along the line or perhaps a Johnson sired one of them."

"That's quite a story you have there, young man. Anyway, so you want to work with us? You want to be involved in private investigations?"

"Private investigations, sir?"

"Yes, detective work. It's a rewarding job but, of course, it can be challenging as well."

"Private investigations?"

"The pay isn't bad at all and the work is full of adventure."

"Private investigations?"

"Why do you keep asking that? You sound like a parrot."

The cold in the room got worse and Latif was almost freezing, the drone of the air conditioning system was getting louder and more irritating to his ears, and the lights in the room continued to blind and hurt his eyes.

It took will for him to focus. Private investigations? Is that what the firm did? "I thought this was a law firm," Latif said.

"Now, where did you get that idea? Did Anna tell you that when you called about the position?"

"No, sir, but..."

"There are no buts about that, young man. We do other things, but primarily we are a private detective firm of sorts. People hire us to investigate people and situations. I mean all kinds of people and all kinds of situations. You name it, we've handled it, from cheating husbands and wives, drug peddlers, crime syndicates, prostitution rings..."

Latif heard Mrs. Doherty's voice echoing: *Mostly gunshots and stabbings.*

Latif folded his arms in an attempt to keep warm, but then the drone of the air conditioning system was so loud now that he had to unfold them to cover his ears. Even worse, the lights in the room were hurting his eyes so badly that he now covered his eyes with his hands. But he thought this was rude, so he brought his hands to his sides.

"Hold on," Mr. Doherty said as he picked up a ringing phone. "Yes. Of course, we will pay. Just give us a little time. The powdered stuff. You know they're not buying as they used to with the cops sniffing around. We don't want to get careless and get busted." He paused and then continued, "No, the rivals won't take over." Another pause. "Sure, we had some attacks—the bastards even took out Tim, but we've got things under control now." He paused again before saying, "Okay, I will see you later."

We do other things...Powdered stuff... Cops sniffing...rivals...busted...took out.... Latif's stomach churned.

"Now, where was I? Mr. Doherty asked. "Oh, yes, the job. We are like a family here, you know. If we decide to hire you, we will take you through special training to make sure you belong and that you can handle the job and that you are reliable. If you pass the test, you too will become part of the *family...*"

Family? Latif thought. You mean, family as in *till death us do part*? He thought of Akos, of his promise to marry her, of walking down the aisle in a tuxedo, she sparkling in one of those glamorous wedding dresses.

Mostly gunshots and stabbings.

Latif closed his eyes, soothed by the relative darkness those closed eyelids offered. After a short while, that darkness seemed to get deeper.

Let's get out of here!!! I think they are coming!!!

63

And then Latif noticed that Mr. Doherty was not speaking and that he had not spoken for a while. Latif opened his eyes and realized that the lights were completely out and the room was plunged into total darkness. Was this some sort of sudden power outage? "Mr. Doherty!" Latif called. When he received no response, he groped his way out of the office and into the corridor, which was also swallowed by incredibly dense darkness, darkness like he had never experienced before. The place was even more silent than earlier. "Mr. Doherty!" Latif called again. Still, there was no response. Latif felt himself being swallowed and attacked by the darkness, as if it had hands jabbing at him and then enfolding his neck in a strangulating hold. "Mrs. Doherty!" he called. There was no response. "Mr. Rodgers! Mr. Upchurch! Mr. Gross! Mr. Sorensen! Anybody!" No response. This confirmed to Latif that the building was empty. In his mind, a voice echoed a warning: *Let's get out of here!!! I think they are coming!!!* It was only at that moment that Latif discerned that it was Mr. Doherty's voice and that it had issued this warning earlier at a moment when Latif had ignored it.

Latif ran through the darkness, using the mental map of the place as drawn by memory. He pushed the door with as much force as he could muster and then the door opened and he was standing outside and the oppressive heat and sunlight bathed him and this time he was glad about that, comforted in their familiar warmth. And when he looked into the distance, he saw Mrs. Doherty and five other men running away. Latif heard distant sounds of the sirens of police cars. He looked to his left and then to his right, and he too began to run away from the building into the vast space of embracing sunlight and encircling heat.

CHAPTER FOUR

***

A Day in the Life

The alarm clock startled Kwaku awake at exactly 5 a.m., as it had for most days the past twenty years. But the deep stupor of sleep drained very slowly from his body as he mumbled almost involuntarily at what he considered to be truncated sleep. After snoozing twice, he finally left his bed twenty minutes later and walked with a lugubrious gait to the bathroom, still fighting the haze that usually plagued him on weekday mornings. He ought to get more sleep, he resolved, knowing that it was a futile resolution, as he remembered most weeknights were identical to the previous night: he had come home at 9 p.m., barely managed to say goodnight to the sleepy children, ate, watched the late news for ten minutes, and worked till 11:30. He had tossed in bed for another forty-five minutes as he wondered how he would be able to make a dent in, let alone complete, his workload.

As he shaved, he tried to veer his thoughts from that mountainous pile of work awaiting him in the office. It was only Tuesday and already the week promised to be strenuous. He was behind on several projects, but his boss kept adding new ones and dictating which ought to be prioritized. In the meantime, many of his clients were calling him and complaining, some even questioning his competence. He realized that he was failing in his effort to minimize thoughts about work only when he cut himself with the shaving blade.

He swore when he saw the tiny trickle of blood on his chin, doubly angered that his body wasn't cooperating. He considered a few stretching exercises to energize his body but, at forty-five, he felt as if his energies had waned beyond recapture. On days such as these—which were lately outnumbering days that weren't as these—he remembered when he did fifty pushups and sixty sit-ups every morning and jogged three miles three times a week. Nowadays, he considered himself lucky if he could go jogging two miles once a week. And he never did any pushups. The muscles that once defined his arms and belly had vanished from sight under an envelope of fat and his once flat belly was beginning to grow a paunch.

Nor could he even find morning sustenance in his marriage. For a few years after his marriage to Akua, he had drawn joy in waking to his wife and replaced morning thoughts of work with thoughts of their marriage, relived images of them together, nights of abandon, including their weeklong honeymoon in Kingston, Jamaica. With a smile, he would shave in those days with vigor, as if shaving off any worries that had accumulated from the previous day. He would call his wife as soon as he arrived in the office and hearing her speak would put him at greater ease to confront the day's tasks. But after twelve years of marriage and two children, even those images had worn thin and the ones they'd recreated over the course of time lacked the verve to overcome the onslaught of work and the fatigue of his ageing body. Now, he shaved without energy, brushed his teeth and bathed without joy.

When he walked back to the bedroom to dress, Akua was awake. "Good morning, Sweetie," she said. He responded in kind, and he meant what he said—about her sweetness—as he knew she meant hers. Sometimes, though, when he realized that the enthusiasm had ebbed, he was guilt-ridden. Akua deserved more than he was giving. She gave him little cause to complain. Yes, she got on his nerves from time to time, but that was rare, typically in moments when his spirits were down and he became easily irritable.

Perhaps it was just that the novelty had dissipated after so many years of marriage and the thrill was gone with time, the pleasures and the memories tossed into the dustbin of familiarity. Perhaps it was just that he was getting older and what pleased him in the past didn't anymore. He would have thought that the waning pleasures of marriage would segue into the pleasures of childrearing—and in a way they had. He was sure to always look at the photo of his family on his desk in the office for occasional sustenance. Mavis and Peter were both smiling in the most recent photo. He couldn't have asked for better children—as if a perfect wife produced perfect children. At eight and six respectively, they were turning into intelligent, articulate, respectful children. Of course, that could belie the coming teenage years that had proved turbulent for many of the families he knew in the neighborhood

But those photo-derived pleasantries, and even joyous times spent with the children, were fleeting. For some reason, it seemed they did not have the staying power of the memories he lived in earlier years of the physical intimacies between he and Akua. Nor could they withstand for long the onslaught of pressures at work.

He smiled at Akua, still trying hard to infuse some energy and joy into the early morning. "You look happy this morning," she said as she stretched her body fully under the covers. "What's the secret?"

"You, of course," he replied unconvincingly.

"Hmmm."

He could never fool her. He dressed quickly, as if he wanted to escape this minor transgression against her.

"Have a nice day, Sweetie," he bid and received the same wish from her.

He went downstairs to prepare his coffee and toast, almost invariably his choice for breakfast. Akua would be up in about an hour, he knew. Now that school was out, she might take the children to the park down the street. As he ate the toast and drank the coffee, he considered taking the day off. He even fantasized, with envy, becoming a teacher like Akua so he could have long vacations to spend with the family. He imagined the summer day's glorious sun as noon, Akua and the children on the park's grass eating sandwiches or perhaps playing Frisbee, the leisurely walk of the neighbors, the chirping of the pigeons…. But he knew these were flimsy thoughts as they needed his income to meet their bills, especially the mortgage payments and property taxes, which ate up about half of their household income. Nor could he realistically take the day off, considering the amount of work he had to complete by day end.

As Kwaku drove to work he turned on the radio to the local public station for the latest news, but he was unable to focus as his phone started ringing. Checking the caller ID he realized it was his mother. He checked the time. It was only 7 a.m. His heart beat hard. She rarely called this early. Could there be some bad news? He picked up.

"What's the matter, Mom?"

"Oh, Kwaku, haven't I taught you any better? Is this the way to answer your phone?"

"It's just that it's so early…"

"Sorry to bother you this early," his mother said. "I know it's early in Chicago, but I needed to remind you to send the money right away."

"Oh, Mom, you had me worried, calling so early. I just haven't had time to go to the bank, but I will send it as I promised."

"I don't want you to forget. I need it. We have nothing left."

"I won't forget, Mom. I will try and do it today, if I can."

"Why can't you just do it? I don't like this *if I can* part."

"I will be very busy today, Mom. I don't know if I will be able to take a break to go to the bank.'

"Huh? Don't tell me you won't take a break for lunch."

"I may not be able to, and even if I do, I will have to work at my desk."

"You must eat lunch no matter how busy you are. I don't want you getting sick. If they are overworking you so much, then find another job or come back home where we will treat you as a king. Have you forgotten that you have a master's degree in accounting?"

"Come back to Ghana, Mom? You know I can't do that now."

"And why not? Are you and Akua not Ghanaian?"

"Yes, we are, but it's not that easy. I went to college here and I've been working here for such a long time. You know I've been away from Ghana for about twenty-six years now. I can't just pack bag and luggage and come to Ghana.'

74

"Oh, yes, you can. If you had built a house here as I asked you to, it would be waiting for you and you could just come and live in it. You and Akua and the children."

"And that's something else, my children were born here."

"And so?"

"I can't just uproot them from their friends and bring them to Ghana. This is their country."

"They are little children. They will adapt to life anywhere. All you need to do is build the house and come and live in it."

"Mom, I can't build a house in Ghana just like that. I've told you several times that I have obligations. I have a mortgage to pay, my school loans, the children's care..."

"Yes, I have heard that several times, but your own friend John has already built two houses..."

"Ma, don't compare me to John. He's a businessman, he doesn't have school loans to pay off..."

"All I hear from you are excuses. At this rate you will rot I America."

"Ma, I will send you the money this week. I have to go."

"I will have to tell your father to talk to you about this."

After his mother hung up, Kwaku almost rear-ended the car in front of him out of a vehicular acceleration stemming from anger. But perhaps it was also partly due to his failing eye-sight. His once perfect vision had become blurry recently and he could not see far objects. He ought to have his eyes checked for near-sightedness. He would do it the coming weekend, he resolved. But as he moved the car forward he remembered he had to attend the children's soccer games on Saturday morning and attend a friend's wedding in the afternoon/evening. And then on Sunday he had church service in the morning and a funeral of a friend's father in the evening.

His phone rang again. It was his friend Joshua. "Man, when are you going to send the money?"

"Joshua," Kwaku said between sighs, "I have told you to wait until next month. I just don't have the money right now."

"Don't give me that crap, Kwaku. A whole accountant telling me he has no money."

"Joshua, we agreed we would incorporate and start operations in six months. Why the hurry?"

"Time waits for no man, my brother. That's six months of lost opportunity. I'm telling you, the trucking business is hot right now. We must do this right away."

"We will do it when I have the money. Bye.'

Deep breaths, honey, he recalled the advice that Akua always gave him when he tensed up. He obeyed her voice and found some calm returning to him.

How could he explain to his mother or Joshua that, although he earned a six-figure salary, when he took out taxes and other payroll deductions, paid the house mortgage and property, which took about half of his monthly income, paid the car payments and insurance on his car, and the electricity and water bills, there was hardly anything left. They had to pay the remainder of their expenses, including groceries, from Akua's salary. How could he make his mother understand that it took sacrifice for him to send her the periodic remittances for her and his father's upkeep? How could he explain to her that he just didn't have the funds to build a house in Ghana? She just wouldn't believe him, always comparing him to this or another person. If even Joshua, who lived in Chicago and was privy to the financial demands of the system, could not see this, then how could he expect his mother to do so?

Deep breaths.

He felt tired by the time he arrived in the office. He realized that his boss' secretary had left him a pile of additional paperwork to be completed with the note; Jim wants to see you first thing in the a.m. It seemed the note had been left the previous night. So when had the boss (Jim Clarke) and his secretary (Joy York) left the office? The man was a workaholic. Recently divorced—no wonder since he was actually married to his work—Jim Clarke arrived in the office early and left late, almost always past 10 p.m. It seemed he wanted to push everyone around him into the same fate.

Kwaku reviewed the paperwork quickly and went to see his boss. He waited outside the boss' office for ten minutes, during which Joy York told him about her plans to go camping for the weekend. When he was let into Jim Clarke's office, the man was reading a pile on his desk. He didn't look up. It was only 8 a.m. but, judging by the level of the coffee in the mug on his desk, the man had already consumed a large quantity of caffeine. "You wanted to see me, sir?" Kwaku asked.

"Kwaku," the mustachioed, bespectacled man said, still without looking up, "I thought I told you I needed the report on the VC Account last night."

"Last night, sir?" Kwaku remembered differently. "Sir, I thought you said you needed it today."

Jim Clarke now looked up at Kwaku, removing his glasses in the process. "Don't give me that. I know what I told you."

"I'm sorry, sir, I am almost done with it. I will have it to you by the end of the day."

"End of the day? Are you for real? You have till midday."

"But..."

"I don't want any excuses. Either you have it to me by midday or I will find someone else who can do it."

"It shall be done, sir."

"It better be."

"And I need a report on the documents Joy left on your desk by the end of the day. And I mean the end of the day   TODAY."

Kwaku was going to have to rush through both jobs, which meant the reports wouldn't be as good as he would have liked, which meant Jim Clarke would rate them poorly, which would definitely affect his upcoming performance review and therefore his raise and any promotion. He needed the pay raise badly to allow some room for spending income for the family and other projects. And he needed the promotion for career advancement. He had been stuck in the same position without a promotion for the past six years. He had tried finding another job but was always told he either didn't have the requisite job experience or that he was over-qualified.

He suppressed these thoughts for the moment and focused on the assignments. He worked through it with as much speed as he could. By midday, he was about three-quarters of the way done with the first assignment. He sweated with worry. He couldn't afford to go downstairs to the cafeteria, but he was so nervous he didn't even feel hungry. Twice when he needed to go to the bathroom, he took his work with him and read as he sat on the toilet. He didn't answer any calls, except Akua's. But all he could tell her was that he couldn't talk and would call her later. He handed in the report at around 2:30. To his relief, Jim Clarke was in a meeting.

As he handed the report to Joy, he asked, "Is he mad?"

"He has been in a foul mood."

Kwaku knew that his boss was even more likely to be angry over the lateness of the report and its quality. He knew it wasn't his best work, but what could he do?

The cafeteria was closed, so he realized he would have to work hungry. If only they had one of those vending machines, he would at least buy some candy. He now turned his attention to the other assignment due by the end of the day. By 4 o'clock he was really hungry and his concentration level was low. He looked at the photo of his family on his desk, but he was too anxious to derive any joy from it. He forced himself to concentrate. By 7 p.m., his eyes hurt and his stomach was growling, but he was only half-way through his task. He considered asking Jim Clarke for an extension, but refrained. His concentration was even lower and the next two hours were a mighty fight as he read words that seemed to swim on the page. By 10 p.m., he could barely write as he prepared the report, his energy level so low he thought he might pass out. When he left the report on Jim Clarke's desk at 11:30, Kwaku moved so slowly and his head ached so strongly he wasn't sure he could drive home. He chewed gum and sang songs to stay awake on his drive home, even if the songs came softly on account of his weakness.

It was only when he arrived home that he realized he hadn't called Akua as he'd promised. She was upstairs, but had left him some *jollof* rice in the microwave—one of the few comforts of the day: being able to eat his favorite dish, a taste acquired and maintained from his days in Ghana.

He checked on his children when he went upstairs. They were both asleep. When he arrived in his bedroom, the lights were off. He tried to be quiet, hoping to slip into bed without waking Akua. But she wasn't asleep.

"You said you would call me back," she said. He knew she wasn't angry, just disappointed. She was rarely angry.

"I'm sorry, honey. I got so busy."

"Too busy to call your wife?"

"I'm sorry, you know how it gets sometimes."

"Hmmm."

He slipped into the bed beside her and kissed her on the cheek. "Goodnight," he said.

"Won't you even ask me what we did today?"

"I'm tired, dear…"

"This is your family, Kwaku. Doesn't it bother you that you have no idea what we did the whole day?"

And he knew that he would have to listen to her for at least another half-hour. It was past midnight and all he wanted to do was fall asleep to relieve the headache still pounding at him. As Akua began to talk about parks and gardens, Kwaku could only close his eyes and imagine.

CHAPTER FIVE

***

Afternoon Delight

I remember the afternoon he came to our village.

I was skeptical at first. At age fifty, I'd seen many of them come riding the high tide of our hopes only to see those hopes smashed. I'd promised myself I wouldn't fall for the seduction this time. But Ama—and others who'd gone to the city and seen or heard of him—was infested with the fever he carried. "This one is different," they insisted. "He is the one." Given my confidence in my wife of twenty-five years, I eventually decided to believe.

It was with hope that we gathered the entire family, including our seven children, to go see him. They too needed the medicine of hope, we decided.

It was a hot day, I tell you. Sunrays seemed to create blazing waves that washed over everything. It became clear to me how special he must be because, despite this heat, the crowd at the town park was unbelievably large. We had to wait for three hours (of heat and sweat), which caused improperly washed armpits to emit smells that I didn't like. But as he was "the one," we suffered patiently.

A motorcade preceded his arrival. We strained our necks to try and see him as ten men dressed in red suits stepped out of three cars, with two motorbikes on the side. "I don't see him," Ama said. It turned out that this was just the first battalion of his entourage. Two more motorcades of identical composition—except one brought gold-dressed men and the other carried green-dressed men—arrived before his appearance. Those in his motorcade, when it arrived, were dressed in myriad forms of red, gold and green. Even though I'd never seen him before, I could distinguish him from the others when he stepped out of his car. He was the only one dressed in a black suit. His entourage quickly formed two long lines from his car to the center of the village park so that he was well flanked as he made his way there. And what a figure he cut as he strolled on slowly, taller than any in his entourage. I was impressed.

He took the spotlight after a long introduction that lasted almost an hour, which mentioned his degrees (about five, if memory serves, including two doctorates), his long list of government jobs held at home and abroad (at least ten), and the organizations to which he belonged (no less than twenty). If there were any remnants of doubt left, the catalogue of accolades erased them. "This man is a god," I whispered to Ama.

We were all cheering loud and hard when it came his turn to speak. He took his time, smiling and nodding as our applause rose, fell and rose. And then there was total silence (except for his voice) when he started speaking: even bleating goats stopped bleating and barking dogs turned quiet when the boom of his voice sounded. If there'd been any lions there, they would have stifled their roars.

"The greatness of the ssendnilbism shall set us free," he announced. "Our ssendnilbism shall equate progress. If you believe in ssendnilbism let me hear you say yes."

"Yes!!!"

The crowd was agog, each one of us trying to outdo the other with enthusiasm.

"Let me here you say ssendnilbism."

We all yelled: "Ssendnilbism!!!"

The next half-hour was a continual chant of "yes" and "ssendnilbism."

We were each full of his sweet fever. He deserved more than our applause, I decided. As we were already standing, I was disappointed we couldn't give him a standing ovation. To remedy this, I started jumping and clapping and soon the entire crowd had joined me in offering him our jumping ovation. Even as he left, we were still yelling "ssendnilbism," his parade of cars and motors vanishing from our view in the horizon and then swallowed within the sunset.

"What a great man," we were all saying as we headed back to our homes.

When I was alone with Ama, I said to her, "I am so impressed. The only thing I need to understand is ssendnilbism. What does it mean?"

With a frown, Ama asked, "You mean you don't understand it either? I thought you knew what it meant."

"No, I thought *you* knew what it meant."

We looked at each other, now a notch wiser, and in every home, we could imagine a similar conversation unfolding. Ama shook her head.

"Well," I said, "even if we don't understand what it means, we can rest assured that when tomorrow comes, the sun will rise again. I only hope we are alive tomorrow

CHAPTER SIX

***

The Executioner's Confession

Madam, may I join you once again? I know it's late, but please indulge me. I need to divulge to you the weight that I am carrying. I can no longer bear it alone. I fear that if I continue to keep it to myself my unshed tears and my souring blood will erupt to cause destruction all around me. I may be speaking as if the words are coming from my head, but this matter bears no intellectualizing. My head may help manufacture the words, but it derives its ingredients from my heart. Sometimes I think I feel too much and other times I believe I think too much. Madam, I am confused....

Yes, I just want to talk. I am in no mood for anything else. Not tonight. Not tonight.

The last time we met I told you about a man scheduled for execution. Do you remember? I mentioned that he was innocent of the crime he was convicted of and that I was praying he would receive a pardon or be granted another trial. Well, the courts turned down his request for a retrial and the president refused to issue a pardon or commute his sentence.

You ask me how I know of his innocence. Well, I can't say that I know. I can only say that I believe. Heart over mind. I have performed many executions, mind you. After a while, you develop a smell for these things—call it a sixth sense, if you will. You can smell the guilty ones from the innocent ones just by being around them, talking to them, reading the map of guilt or innocence in the eyes. But don't take my word for it. The man himself insisted on his innocence and never wavered. Of course, as many a condemned man professes innocence, I know we ought to look for objective indications. So how about the opinion of just about every lawyer and human rights advocate of renown in the country? You have seen them, haven't you?

I'm talking about the demonstrations organized by the human rights groups, and the countless legal practitioners who have voiced their opinions on the matter. Oh, you know how they have demonstrated under the scorching sun and held vigil deep into the unmentionable hours of the night.

To any fair minded person, this is clearly a case of justice miscarried. Do you remember the facts of the matter? Let me remind you.

It is undisputed that in the dawn hours of one Saturday, someone, armed with a gun, broke down the locks of Mr. Afari's residence, shot him and made away with a stash of cash. We all knew when we heard of the murder and robbery that there would be a public outcry for justice. Mr. Afari, after all, was one of the most outstanding and sympathetic figures of our times—a man paralyzed from the waist down who rode his hand-propelled tricycle across the country seeking donations for charitable foundations. You remember how much attention he garnered and how he was featured on national and international media and bestowed with many awards. You recall that after many heard of him he was held aloft as a national hero and often invited to give honorarium-paid speeches.

Many would not consider him rich, but in the Nima neighborhood where he continued to live, he would have been deemed quite privileged, given his newly bestowed fame and relative wealth. This was bound to generate attention and envy. I'm sure many of his neighbors would kill for a fraction of what he managed to achieve. It's unfortunate that someone actually acted on jealousy or covetousness to rob and kill him. And what an outcry for justice erupted after his death. I can still remember the packed marketplace where rallies were held and vociferous calls made for the perpetrator to be captured.

Amid the public uproar, the police had to act quickly and decisively. They arrested the man, a renowned robber, also reputed for past murders, on the word of an elderly neighbor who claimed to have seen the man enter Mr. Afari's home and rush out minutes later. This thickly bespectacled neighbor was eighty-five years old and barely coherent. Based on his account and the discovery of the man's fingerprints in the deceased's residence, the police arrested the man and the government brought him to trial. Talk about circumstantial evidence and bad circumstantial evidence at that. Oh, and I'm sure you remember the demonstrations that mushroomed all over the city when the man was arrested. Students and workers, old and young alike, were all over the place bellowing and carrying placards calling for his execution.

In that kind of environment, I sometimes don't blame the overzealousness of the police. Indeed, it was an atmosphere that promoted recklessness. In their eagerness, they focused solely on the man once he was fingered by their witness, ignoring evidence that surfaced later. I'm talking about other witnesses who provided the man with an unshakable alibi that he was with them in a bar at the time of the murder. I'm talking about a woman who came forward later to testify that another man, a notorious robber, had confessed to him that he killed Mr. Afari. Unfortunately, by the time she came forward, that robber had absconded. Some say he fled to a neighboring country, where he was himself killed in a bar brawl. If anyone doubted the woman's claim, their doubts should have dissipated when she pointed them to where the robber buried the murder weapons. But it appeared the robber had cleaned it of all prints.

You would think the prosecutor would exercise some tampering influence over proceedings in the face of such potentially exculpatory evidence. But no. He, also engulfed in the city-wide madness, ignored the evidence and argued for the death penalty. Of course, the defense introduced the alibi at trial and the testimony of the woman, against the prosecutor's objection of hearsay. But the prosecutor's cross-examination of the woman revealed that she was a prostitute, which the prosecutor used to insinuate that her testimony was not to be believed. Madam, I hope you don't take offense at that. And what of the testimony of all those who provided the alibi, you ask? Well, the prosecutor claimed they were all lying to help a friend. Who, he said, would believe the testimony of a "bunch of drunkards"? The defense counsel objected to such characterization, but whatever harm the prosecutor intended to inflict was already done.

Even many in the public at large who believed that the accused didn't kill Mr. Afari called for a guilty verdict anyway. Hadn't he robbed others before? Hadn't he killed others in the past and gotten away with it? It was society's payback time for his crimes, whether or not proven, against humanity.

I don't think I'm saying these things because I am faint-hearted. Let me remind you that I have presided over many executions. Although all of them have taken a toll, none has affected me like this one. Or it could be that things have just accumulated and I am finally breaking under the weight. Let me tell you a little more. Please bear with me.

They had scheduled the execution for midnight. For those executions, I usually leave home around 11 p.m. This time, I did not wait for the clock to chime before I set out. I was anxious, my mind wondering, now prodding me to go forth and accomplish my duty, now urging me to stay at home and not taint myself any further with the scheduled killing. I was unsettled, my mind wandering over my life for the past twenty years or so, thinking I had accomplished much with all that I had done for country and justice and in the next instant convinced that I had thrown away my times into the dustbin of vengefulness. In my living room, the clock's pendulum swung back and forth, as if pleading the case of my uncertainty amid the certainty of the death sentence. For a while I was immobilized by the contradictions—anxious to get to the scene of the execution, while at the same time hoping that it would not happen, hoping that time would skip this particular moment so that I would find myself on its other side where the execution had already taken place without my participation.

You may wonder why I didn't just refuse to carry out the sentence or simply resign my job if I had such a problem with the man's guilt. The answer is not so simple. As I think about it, I attribute it to compassion and duty.

You seem to bristle at the word compassion.

Why the compassion? I have been at this job such a long time that I think I came to believe I could bring a more compassionate approach to the execution—more so than any executioner who might believe the man was guilty. I would be there to carry out the sentence, yes; but I would also provide all the support I could give, if such a thing was at all possible in a man's last hours. I would be able to utter encouraging words to him, comforting words that might lessen the gravity of his fate. With my years of experience, I was convinced I could summon sufficient calm do this. And then there was that sense of duty. It was my job and a man doesn't run from his job when it gets difficult. Simple as that. This was what I was tasked to do, and been tasked to do since the day I was appointed executioner.

That itself was a journey—the job.

I'd heard of executions from time to time, but remained indifferent to them. In fact, I didn't think government executions were a matter deserving of my attention. Let the government do its business and let me worry about mine. That was my philosophy, if you will.

After secondary school and a series of short-lived jobs as an office messenger and then a loading clerk at the harbor, I was unfulfilled. Was this how I was going to spend the rest of my life? Not that I was a particularly bright student, but I could have made it to the university if only we were a bit richer. Forced to start working earlier than I'd hoped, I was eager to find a more fulfilling job. For years I searched and waited. And then the *perfect* job found me.

I lost my agnosticism for the death penalty when my father was murdered. You may be too young to remember that famous case of a brutal murder committed in broad daylight. You see, my father was a security guard at a bank when armed robbers attacked it. The first thing the robbers did was shoot him. It was an efficient operation and they removed the first clog before it could become a bigger impediment. The cruelty of it was that it didn't matter to them that he was a human being with a wife and children, a family that cared for him. That much was evident during the trial of the four robbers. I couldn't have been happier that they each received the death penalty.

But I felt so unfulfilled after they were executed. It felt so sudden, so unsatisfying. Because the government had refused my request to witness the execution, I had not seen their faces as they were walked to the dangling noose, the unmask-able fear that I hoped would register in their faces as they faced death. Whenever I felt the pain of my father's death, I wished that I had been the one who kicked the support from under their feet and heard their last gasps in the violence of death, its sweet triumph over them. This wish lived with me day and night. It became a part of me, one with my pulse, until I had to find a way to release its demands on me. The best way I could think of doing this was by becoming a prison guard, which I hoped would bring me close enough to be witness to the hopeless plight of the condemned, which I hoped would offer me an opportunity to torment them any way I could.

I worked hard at it when I got the job, acquiring a reputation as a mean guard. I mocked the prisoners and beat them when I got the least opportunity. And then after a few years I volunteered for an opening as a hangman. It seemed not many people wanted it, but I had a mission. I got the job after a short period of training, which comprised learning the procedure of executions—the proper way to tie the noose and things like that. Easy stuff. I was only thirty years old at that time, just about to get married. I considered this a great promotion and a mighty blessing.

And how thrilling it was the first time I prepared the noose. It was only a week after my wedding. Newly married, full of joy and the bliss of a five-day honeymoon, here I was tasked with hanging a murderer. My wife worried that I wouldn't be able to go through with it. How wrong she was.

When the clock chimed eleven, I left home and went to the prison. I prepared the noose and placed a wooden box underneath it, all the while thinking of my father. The more I thought of how he'd died, the more exhilarated I became. When I went, together with a couple of guards to fetch the convicted from his room, I was so thrilled I was even grinning. You should have seen the man's face. I don't know if I've seen a sadder and more scared face in my life, with its drooped cheeks and lips and wide-opened eyes that held nothing but fear. Our eyes locked for a moment and he seemed surprised that I was so gleeful.

His body shook violently as the guards took him by the hand and then tears generously began falling down his cheeks. No one said anything to him as we led him to the execution room. To mock him, and I consider this my signature, I pushed the noose ever so lightly so that it swung back and forth like a pendulum. (I have performed this pendulous-tease ever since for all whom I have executed.) I grinned wider before I put the hood over his head. I wanted him to see how much I enjoyed it. And I laughed as I kicked the box from underneath his feet and as his body strained into its demise. I was so invigorated by this feat. In a way, I felt I had begun to avenge my father's murder. I saw each murderer as my father's killer. And I imagined my father applauding from his grave with each one I put to death in the execution room.

But, something strange began to happen to me. After the thrill of the first few hangings, I realized that I was no longer deriving the same level of pleasure from them. The pleasure had increased at an increasing rate and then, after a while, with each successive execution, the joy increased at a decreasing rate and eventually began to diminish. What do economists call it? The Law of Diminishing Returns, or something like that. In my case you could call it the Law of Diminishing Joyous Executions.

Worse, something even stranger began to happen to me. Not only did I no longer feel joyous and thrilled by the executions as before, but I also began to see those that I had killed. You don't believe me? I swear it's true. I can't say with certainty exactly when it started. It must have been around the time my first child was born. I was about thirty-five when she was born. She must have been about three months old when I returned from an execution. In the dawn hours, as I slept, I heard her cry and then I woke up and I swear the dead man's face was hovering over me. I yelled and woke up my wife.

104

"What's the matter," she asked, as she ran to our child, thinking something was wrong with her.

"Nothing," I said and pretended to return to asleep.

But I couldn't sleep the remainder of that dawn. This appearance would happen a couple of times more until the next execution and then there were two faces appearing before me in my sleeping hours. By the time our second child, my son, was born, I not only saw them in my sleeping hours but also sometimes when I was awake and alone. I was about forty years around then. It could happen anywhere—whether in the toilet, bedroom, or office—the faces of the dead just before I hooded them appearing and disappearing and reappearing. As you can imagine, after these haunts, I no longer grinned or laughed come execution time. I just performed the job as quickly as I could. The only luxury I continued to offer myself was the pendulous tease.

And I took to drinking. And when I say drinking, I mean heavy drinking. I started with a little here and a little there to help me cope with the dead men's visitations. Whenever I was inebriated, it was easier for me to dismiss them; conversely, I was having a harder time with them when I was sober. For that reason, I started drinking almost all the time.

My wife started complaining about my drinking and its accompanying irresponsibleness—refusing to bathe for days, spending large amounts on alcohol, and not contributing to the upkeep of the house. I insulted her when she kept complaining. She asked some elders to speak reason to me. I insulted them also. After a while, when all her complaints failed to effect any change, she left and took the children with her.

You know, I knew what I was doing was wrong, but I took so much comfort in the oblivion from the haunts that the alcohol provided me that I couldn't stop. And so I kept at it, and it even got worse after she left. I was fifty at that time—strange that she was able to accommodate me for so long. As I may have told you before, I am now fifty-three. I only come to this place because a man has his needs, you know. Without a wife, what should I do? I don't think any woman would want to marry me in my current condition.

But to return to the matter at hand, as you can see, I have had a long stretch of experience killing people. I have reached an internal resolution with myself that I will finish my job, which has become a sentence of its own, go on pension and live as peaceably as I can with my bottles and the faces of the dead as I await my own death. Call it a bargain with reality, if a sad one.

And then this case came along.

I was so anxious that—as I have said—I left house before the clock chimed. In recent times, I drank a glassful of gin before I left home and another glassful when I returned. But as I reached for the bottle, my hand kept shaking so badly that I could barely hold it. I withdrew my hand and tried again. The shaking was even worse. After this happened the third time, I decided to forgo the drink. For me, this was a major defeat. Or perhaps it was a great feat.

When I stepped outside of my house, the air was suffocating. If a gazillion tear drops had gathered in the air to make it so humid, it would be all too befitting for the innocent head about to be hanged. Of course, if you believe the man guilty of other murders, then the word innocent might seem out of place. But, whether or not he had killed before, he was innocent of the crime for which he had been sentenced to die.

I walked in the heavy air, on the empty streets. I found it difficult to breathe, as the oppressing air filled my lungs.

Murderer, I could hear a voice say in my ears. If I wasn't mistaken, this voice was that of the first man I executed. *Murderer*, another voice said, and then another, and then another, each distinct and each belonging to someone from the past that I had executed. I wanted to protest this charge, but alone in the streets at that hour, what good would it do? I would just manage the voices, I decided. But then I heard another one, louder and clearer and more distinct than any of the others. And it spoke with the accusatory vividness of the living. It was the voice of the man I was about to execute, also accusing me of being a murderer. I could decide not to respond to the dead, but the living? "I am only doing my job," I said, but his voice continued to rise above the others in clarity as he continued to accuse me.

I halted and considered returning home. I looked to my left and to my right, in front and behind me. Except for the few soft glows of lit bulbs in houses here and there, the long stretch of the road before me was lightless and deserted. Even the moon had disappeared. A sound or two would have helped calm my nerves; but no, it was a silent as the catacombs at night, except for the running gutters transporting dead vermin, sewage and other wastes. I moved on, resolved that I had to do my job, despite my reservations.

One step forward and I stepped into something mushy. I didn't have to be told that it was shit. I cursed those who deemed it fit to defecate on the road. We hadn't had running water in about a week, so it wasn't surprising that some would do this outside, but could they not have found a better place than this? I rubbed my shoe several times on the dirt ground to get rid of the feces. Eventually, I think I did, but the stinging smell of offensively smelling excrement remained with me. A few steps forward and I

109

stepped into something hard. When I checked, I realized it was a piece of broken bottle. I noticed that a portion of the road was littered with more of the same. Thank God I was wearing thick soled shoes. Even if the broken piece had caused some damage to the soles of my shoes, I hadn't suffered physical injury. After a few more steps, I came into view of a number of mango trees that lined the rest of the road. Looking at them, I noticed a number of bats perched on their branches, hanging upside down, some with eyes that seemed to glitter in the dark. I cringed, afraid that they would attack me at any moment. I walked the rest of the lightless path with caution, accompanied by the smell of shit, the threatening presence of bats and the accusing sounds of dead men's voices.

I exhaled with relief when after five minutes I turned the corner and entered the final stretch of the way, which had streetlights and no bats. Still, the smell and voices stayed with me, the voices leaving only when, after about another half-hour walk, I arrived at the prison.

I moved slowly, hoping that by some miraculous turn of events, the condemned man would get some reprieve—a pardon or commutation of his sentence—anything to remove this burden from me, this tightening noose around my neck.

I didn't want to kill him, but....

I tied the noose very slowly, the other guards urging me to hurry as the appointed time had drawn near. If they could smell the shit, they didn't say. I refused to go to the room with the other guards to fetch him as had been the protocol of this particular prison. Even when they brought him to the execution room, I didn't want to look at him, forced to do so out of necessity. As he stepped forward to the poles where the noose dangled, he looked at me while I prepared to put the hood over his head. I would not do the pendulous tease this time.

"I did not commit this crime," the man said.

At that moment, I wanted to find solace in the belief that even if he hadn't committed this particular murder, he had committed others and was therefore not innocent. But was that then to say that any one deserved to die for whatever crimes he may have committed even if they'd not been proved to have committed them? I wasn't sure I was prepared to follow that kind of reasoning at that time.

But what could I say? I know you are innocent? For what purpose? Would he not then be justified in asking me, why I was participating in his death?

"Be brave," was all that I could say.

The man looked at me and I could see his eyes fatten with tears. I could see them pleading. I tell you, if I hadn't looked away from his eyes I may very well have bolted from the room. I moved very quickly to hood his head. As I did so, my head accidentally touched the noose and it began to swing back and forth. I hooded him immediately. *Die and stop accusing me with the voice of the living*, I yelled in my mind. I barely waited for him to mount the stool before I kicked it from underneath him and his body spoke the prelude of death with its violent struggle. I didn't wait for them to take his body down and pronounce him dead as I have done in the past. I fled the scene, my body seeming to fall apart with increasing trembling, as his voice was added to the voices of the dead, calling after me: *Murderer*.

And, madam, I came to find you. And tonight, I am convinced that my journey towards death, which began a long time ago, grew much slipperier.

CHAPTER SEVEN

***

The Glitter

I had been at my job for a long time. It neither required nor paid much. I usually arrived at work around 9 in the morning, picked up packages of soap at the factory, loaded them into a van, and delivered them to designated customers. Depending on the demand for the day, I often took my lunch around noon and resumed work an hour or so later. I closed from work around 3:30. In the thirteen years since I started working for the company, this routine had varied little and I had settled into it comfortably. In fact, I had become so at ease with it that I must have forgotten that an alternative form of life was even possible.

Although the pay wasn't much and we relied heavily on my wife's income as a seller of footwear in a nearby market, it afforded me plenty of time to spend with my wife of ten years and our five year old son. When I got bored with family life, I spent my evenings with my friends in the nearby kiosks enjoying local firewater, working out lotto numbers, and arguing about politics. Somehow, I knew there was more to life than this, but with nothing more than a primary school education, I was also aware that my options were limited. As it was, my only reach for greater things was limited to the luxury cars I admired on the roads and the mansions in the high class areas of Accra.

I know I shouldn't have picked up that lady. You see, it was a hot afternoon and I was on one of my deliveries when I saw her standing under the scorching sun, waving for a ride. There were no trees to offer her shade at the time of the afternoon—about two hours past noon. As I drove closer, I noticed how sweat poured out of her body. She could certainly use the aid of a ride. I have to admit I was not being altogether altruistic when I stopped to pick her. She was a very attractive lady, slim but curvy.

"Where to?" I asked.

"Drop me at the nearest hotel."

116

"Are you a visitor to the city?"

She smiled coyly at the lips, but her eyes held firm. The combined coyness and brazenness almost unnerved me. And then she rolled her eyes. I swear they seemed to turn like dice. She walked closer, assuredly regal. With see-saw swaying hips, she stepped silently and gently. She stopped and squinted at me. She extended her hand and paused. They were well manicured but I felt like they were claws over my head. Sweat became my face. I was able to extend my hand, but with effort. She moved hers closer; in fact, it seemed she glided it in the air as she touched mine.

"Are you a visitor," I asked again, my voice a bit unsteady.

"I suppose in a manner of speaking you could say that," she said.

She didn't wait for me to invite her in. She walked around the car and opened the unlocked door on the passenger's side and sat down. I smelled her perfume, which remained untainted by her sweat. It had a lime quality to it. I liked it and told her so.

When I started moving the van again, I wasn't looking for any adventure with her. Far from it. My wish was to enjoy her presence, drop her off and be on my way. Not that I wouldn't accept it if other opportunities came, but I didn't expect any. After ten years of marriage, I had come to accept my lot with my wife, who wasn't bad looking herself. She was only twenty when we married and, over time, she had lost some of her attractiveness. But to be honest, she didn't compare with the beauty I picked up.

"I know a hotel around the corner," I said. "It's nice and reasonable."

"That will do."

Suddenly, as she said this, I noticed that, except for her purse, she wasn't carrying anything else. How this had escaped me so far surprised me.

"I thought you were a visitor," I said. "How come you have no bags?"

"I travel light," she said.

I thought this very strange. Perhaps she was no visitor at all. Perhaps she was meeting someone for a tryst.

Still, it didn't make sense. If it was a prearranged meeting, wouldn't she have a specific location in mind when I picked her up? Or was she a prostitute seeking to solicit business at the nearest foraging ground? She didn't seem the type. She wasn't dressed in any tight, revealing dress. In fact, her dress, which reached well below her knees, was a little too loose, I thought. In any case, it was none of my business. I would drop her off and go about the rest of my business, and she would linger in my memories and fantasies for a while and fade like the rest of them that I saw, admired or desired, but knew were beyond my grasp.

"What's all that?" she asked.

"What?"

"The stuff in the back."

"Oh, those are just packages of soap I need to deliver."

"Is that what you do, a delivery man?"

"Yes, that's my job."

"Oh, then why did you stop to pick me up if you're on the job?"

I wasn't prepared for this question and it took me a while to answer. She seized on the pause, for she was smiling unbelievingly at me when I said, "I just wanted to offer some help. I didn't like the way the sun was burning you."

"Is that all?" she said, her smile still intact.

I merely nodded. From my peripheral vision, I could tell she was still looking at me.

"When do you get off from work?" she asked.

"Why do you want to know?"

"Just curious." I maintained my silence. "So are you going to tell me or not?"

"Around three or four."

"That may be too late for him," she said.

"Too late for whom?"

"What time do you break for lunch?"

"Why are you asking me all these questions?"

"Just tell me. I'm doing research."

"Research on what? First you are a visitor and now you are a researcher?"

"Are the two mutually exclusive?"

I didn't respond.

"I tell you what," she said. "Just drive a little farther down the road and let me show you a house. It belongs to my boss. He's looking for a new housekeeper…"

"I am not a housekeeper."

"Trust me, it will be worth your while. He's an old man with lots of money. He will pay you much more in a month than you earn in a year. I guarantee you that."

"I told you I am a driver, a delivery man. I am not a housekeeper."

"Come on, how hard can it be? You dust here a little, clean there a little and you're done. He lives alone, so the house is hardly dirty to begin with."

"This all sounds very strange to me. I just picked you up. You don't know me. How can you ask me to take the job? What if I am a thief? What if I am a murderer?"

"But you are not."

"How do you know?"

"You passed the test. So many cars drove past me without stopping. The drivers that stopped started propositioning me even before they offered me a ride. You are not like them. I can tell wholesomeness when I see it."

"What work do you do for him anyway?"

"I am his secretary. I organize his affairs."

"Is that all?"

"Why do you ask?"

"Just curious?"

She laughed. "Really?"

"Look, lady," I said. "We are almost at the hotel. I'll drop you off and be on my way."

"My name is Aba," she said. "What's yours?"

"Albert," I said.

"You have nothing to lose, Albert" she replied. "Just drive up the street and I'll show you the house. If you are interested, show up tomorrow at noon. I presume like most people you take your lunch break around then. I will tell the Mister about you. If you show up, great; if not, that's fine as well. What I can tell you is that it would be the easiest job you ever had for the most money you've ever made." Her hand glided in the air and touched my thigh as she added, "And there are other perks."

I looked at her. She was smiling. That was when she gave me hope and confidence. I had some reservations about her invitation, but this touch changed the equation. I drove forward to the location she directed. She pointed to the mansion and said, "See you at noon tomorrow," as she stepped out of the van and walked toward it.

The rest of the afternoon, I contemplated the invitation. It sounded too good to be true just as much as it sounded too good to reject. She was right. What did I have to lose? I would skip lunch, show up at noon and see what they had to offer. If I liked it, I would take it; if I didn't like it, I would keep my job. Nor could I ignore that invitation to extramarital adventure that she'd suggested. A little mischief kept in secret could provide some excitement outside of the routine that had made my life so dull. I realized she may have said it without actually intending to act on it. If so, I could still do well with more money.

I showed up at noon the next day. The watchman in the front let me in. "Mister is expecting you," he said.

"How about Aba?"

123

"Madam Aba is not here at the moment," he said, "But she said everything is set. Just go to the front door and ring the bell. Mister will let you in."

Once I stepped onto the compound, I was able to study the building. It was one of those colonial style mansions. It hovered over a two acre land, sitting behind a green-grassed-lawn, but seemed to almost tumble over its own cul-de-sac. It was a three-storey edifice, a massive monument bestriding a subjugated land. The trees that lined the pathway were immaculately aligned, blotting out the sunlight in parts, and the hedges behind it perfectly manicured. No birds chirped. The place was dead silent. I walked its long entryway to the front porch and rang the doorbell. Even from the outside, I could hear it sound—a strident doorbell-performance, if you ask me.

Mister opened the door. His facial features were hidden in massive chunks of flesh on the cheeks and accentuated by a multiple chin. As he stepped back to let me into the living room, I noticed the flesh of pounds hanging from his waist region. As he moved, I was reminded of shaking maraca. I also noticed the ceiling, at

124

least twelve feet high, and the array of glimmering chandeliers.

"Welcome," he said, but disturbance guarded his eyes. "Aba speaks highly of you and I trust her judgment." He paused, as if expecting me so speak, and then added, "She said you could even start today."

"I..."

"Is it the salary that makes you hesitate? Pardon me then, let's talk business first."

He scratched his head and pulled out a notebook from his pocket. He tore out a page and handed it over to me. "This is what we are offering to pay you."

This was an unorthodox way of making an offer, but if I had any reservations, they vanished when I saw the figure on the page. The monthly pay was the equivalent of my yearly compensation at the factory. "What do you say?"

I had no more reservations. "This is perfect."

"Great. You can start with some light work today. Just clean up the bedrooms. Since this is your first day, it will help you familiarize yourself with the place. You can do the rest of the cleaning tomorrow."

I was not about to say that I wasn't ready, that I was not a trained housekeeper. I would learn it. Given the incentive, I just had to.

Mister led me to a storeroom and showed me the cleaning supplies. Then he took me to the topmost floor where the bedrooms were located. Without opening the doors he pointed them out to me and said, "You can get to work, but I have to attend to some business downtown. I hope to be back soon, but in case I'm not back by the time you're done, feel free to let yourself out." He handed me a stash of cash and said, "This is half of your pay for the month. I will pay you two weeks in advance."

With that he left me. In a short while I heard a car leaving the mansion, and I assumed that he was gone. The mansion belonged to me. I counted thirteen bedrooms. I went to the storeroom and gathered what I thought I'd need. I wasn't sure I could clean it to his satisfaction but I would do the best I could and learn from whomever I could in the course of the week.

I picked a room at random to clean on the topmost floor.

The first room I entered already looked immaculate to me. Nothing seemed out of place. Except for some dust on the windows, everything else was clean. I dusted it and moved to the next room. Same story. It was only in the thirteenth room that I noticed the first photograph in the house. And suddenly my blood curdled from the awareness of the absence of livingness— a gaping presence of incompleteness. No voice or body, no laughter or even sob in the house, except now the framed portrait of a young woman hanging on the wall, with hair artificially stretched to her shoulders, and extended into bangs shading a countenanced brow, hair hovering over a weak look hoarded in recessed eyes. I saw grace wrestle with vulnerability. A figurine hanging below it seemed placed there with cognoscente-skill.

I am not sure if what happened next was just from my imagination. As I stared at the photo, the glass held within the frame broke without shattering—a thin crack, a geographic fault, a dawning threat.

I shuddered but sought to unlock the sudden mystery

And then I saw smoke rising from a revolver's muzzle, lifted by listless wind shattered by gun power. Imagination or reality, it became my reality. I, as stunned audience looked, unable to believe the freed scene. A bullet lodged in the young woman's writhing body and she staggered toward me, staring at me in disbelief as the wound in her heart widened. And then she stumbled to the ground to embrace the stillness of death. Suddenly, this vagarious encounter had set a tone that pointed to death and mayhem. And I saw pots of gold break into goblets of blood. Right before my eyes. And the mansion became a fetish to the dead with its quiet and unnatural stillness, with its impression of activity abruptly suspended and even abandoned, conjuring something that filled me with diabolical dread. And I was afraid I was losing something essential. If it were mere physical energy I could recoup it. But this thing sapped internal energies. The voices of death echoed, my nostrils flared—calderas smoldering fear.

128

And then the scene was cleared and all I could see was the portrait with the crack in it. Tears welled up in eyes of the young woman in the portrait and she blinked them down unto her cheeks. And then as if her tears were a mirror I saw Mister. I turned around and he was standing behind me with a revolver at the ready. I could hear the voice of the young woman in the portrait say, "You allowed Aba to entice you. The source of his wealth is in blood, the blood of good men and women. Each drop is worth a million and his gods are famished. You are their sacrifice, as I was. Now you will be had, trapped as a picture-dead, until another comes to replace you, like you me."

I saw the danger clearly, but I could ill afford to negotiate time. I jumped forward into the flesh readying to fire, stumbling him and perhaps stunning him with my daring. I heard gunshots, but I was moving on, zigzagging. I broke open into a bedroom and then jumped out of a window. I wasn't thinking. I just did it, knowing that death was the only alternative. As I fell, I discovered sudden simian ability to swing on the trees on which I landed and subsequently moved. "Don't let him out!" I could hear an order, but, fear being a great inspirer, I was way past the gate even before the watchman could react.

I don't know exactly how I did it, but I gave myself the permission to think only when I was pushing on the accelerator of the van. Call it a miracle. When I checked the time, it was almost three. My next thought was how I was going to explain the undelivered packages to my boss. But, considering what had just happened, I counted myself blessed.

CHAPTER EIGHT

***

The Farewell

I'd need a car to get anywhere from this secluded home. The urge to drink grew stronger when I was introduced to my bare room: a window facing the outside, a bed, a television set, and a ceiling fan. And the place smelled of old people. And it had the feel of death.

I set to explore the place a little when the claustrophobic boredom and desire for booze got too strong. What kind of a home was this? Just about everyone I saw had an ailment and a significant majority was bound to wheelchairs, most with the silent mask of imminent death. And to add to the sense of death was the remoteness of the place—as though to say that the world ought not be bothered by the tales of their lives, that it was better for the denouement to occur silently amid trees and flowers.

In the main hall, a gathering of the nursed was watching old movies. I stared into the gathering, a chill up my spine, the sea of whiteness suggesting, without a word being said, my otherness. No one said it, but I felt unwelcome. After the movie ended, my daughter's friend Nadia came by. As far as I could tell, she was the only black person there, excepting me. I wondered if she'd planned to have me there just to have a little bit of familiarity around. After all, she was the one who suggested to my daughter to put me here. I, too, found comfort in her presence.

"Everything okay?" She asked me.

I need some liquor. Aloud I said, "It will take some getting used to."

"Hang in there." She smiled. "If you need anything, anything at all, let me know, okay? I work the day shift, so you can find me before I leave around five."

I felt cheated the moment she left me. Abandoned. I would've liked to see my daughter there. A man is ready to open and close chapters in his youth, but there comes a time when a familiar chapter becomes the one he wishes to keep opened until the end. But, now, to realize that the anticipated end had become a segue to another unanticipated chapter made reading it too awesome. I retreated to my room in anger. The only hope I could find was the hand of Nadia. Hang in there, she'd said. But whose expectation was that? My daughter Afia? Mine? Nadia's?

I couldn't sleep hours after I tried. A quiet too unsettling for me had come to the place. I liked quiet, but the soulless quiet—this noticeable negation (as opposed to temporary suspension) of sound—was too much. I resolved to challenge it. I stepped outside into it. The porch was dimly lit, leading into the night and woods out there. I sat on a wicker chair on the porch to face the chilly breeze. Again, I looked into the night, which brought to me its full self, like a secretive creature unmasked. But what did the masquerade hold in store for me except to offer the calm for me to converse with myself? And I heard my own voice say *What are you doing here?* And the other reply *I am...* and then lose its focus, whimpering in the breathtaking freefall of its owner, the downward slide from job and wife to jobless, now homeless. The other voice tried to reason *Could it be any worse than what you had before? Shouldn't you be proud that you've been offered this opportunity to escape the humdrum you faced before, the Sisyphian drudgery?* (But isn't Sisyphus supposed to be presumed happy? Or is it a false presumption?) The other voice was trying to wrestle the night's hollowness away and it continued, *Here's your opportunity to create anew that which you hated.*

I didn't hate it.

Come, come, you know you did. Remember the daily waking up, the boredom, tedium and stress of work, a wife you hardly touched, children gone...

That voice had to be stifled. I am a lonely man, I said. Like the day I was born, I am a lonely man. Like my journey in America, I am a lonely man. Who will rescue me? Who will rescue me? Who will guide me through the bleak passages of night? The deep and ~~un~~known and the shallow and ~~un~~known? Linked by the ~~un~~known. I saw no

134

room for compromise. *Stop this self-pity, you're pathetic.*
This is behavior unbecoming.

"Didn't your mama tell you not to sit outside alone in the cold?"

Before I turned to look at the owner of the voice coming from behind me, I reconciled myself to the three words that stood out. Outside. Alone. Cold. What brilliance captured the mood so succinctly and accurately? A pale figure emerged—as pale as they would describe a ghost. Was he a ghost? His voice rang weak, but confident, his walk was deliberate, gingerly and seemingly painful. "Couldn't sleep, huh?"

"No," I said. "Trying to see if this will do any good."

"You're not from these parts, are you?"

"No, why do you ask?"

"Your accent. It sounds foreign."

Foreign? I've been living in the States for thirty-two years or so, a life span for some. Much longer than I've lived anywhere else. "I see." *Oh ghostly man, will you*

too remind me of my alienation, this ubiquitous otherness
that surrounds me like air?

"Wonderful night, ain't it?"

"That it is."

"Name's Ron."

"Kojo."

"Kojo. Where're you from?

America, dammit. "I'm from Ghana."

"Ghana, that's African, ain't it?

"Yes."

"Africa. I've always wanted to go, but never got the chance. I'd have loved a safari, you know, see them animals."

Animals. Animals. Animals. Animals. Animals.
Animals. Animals. Animals. Animals. Animals. Animals.
Animals. Animals. Animals. Animals. Animals. Animals.
Animals. Animals. Animals. Animals. Animals. Animals.
Animals. Animals. Animals. Animals. Animals. Animals.
Animals

Yes, I too was irritated. *There's more to Africa than safaris and animals, you old....*

"Not too late," I said. "Nothing's ever too late."

"At my age? It's hard enough moving from room to room." He coughed an abbreviated cough. "Can't do. Hell, it's a good day when I can get through it without shitting in my pants." Another abbreviated cough. "But you, what's your story? You're too young to come here to die like the rest of us."

Come here to die? "My story. How do you mean?"

"What brings you here? I know it's none of my business but I don't see many of your kind in places like this."

My kind. There we go again. "It's a long story, Ron."

"Fair enough. Oh, well, I'm going back inside and try and get me some sleep. See you in the morning."

After Ron left, I was again left to the night, staring at me, seemingly lifeless, seemingly treacherous. It became clear, the threat it seemed to carry, and the images

137

it carried along to me from Ma's and Pa's ghosts. I cursed my wife Greta for divorcing me after thirty years of marriage, taking away so much, including the house, that I was forced to shack up with my daughter. But Afia had her own life. I couldn't continue to impose.

I needed my liquor.

And the next day I asked Nadia to get me some. But she wouldn't budge. "I promised Afia," she said.

I was angry with her. As I walked away pouting, Ron said, "That doesn't become a grown man like you. Come sit with me a minute, will you?"

We sat silently for several minutes.

"Aaah," Ron gasped when he saw me later that day. "The memories." He eyed me from the corner of his watery eye. "Don't you miss times past? It's the affliction of old age," he said. "But then, again, you're young. I tell you, it ain't easy to bury a wife and a child if you know what I mean. Were you ever married?"

"Yes, but divorced."

"Kids?"

"I have one. A girl."

"Living?"

"Yes."

"You lucky, Kojo. I buried my kid five years ago and my wife just last year."

"Sorry."

"Oh, don't be sorry. It's part of life, but it still hurts like a fresh wound. I tell you what, man. If your kid isn't married, get her married and get some grandkids if you ain't got none. That's your claim to the future... But I talk too much. You're going to the show this afternoon?"

"What show?"

"No one told you? They're having some local band come play at three." Ron coughed. "I'm going to dance with Thelma. Met her yet?"

"No."

"Sweet lady. Come on, I'll introduce you."

Thelma was asleep. But a little later we would learn that she'd died. Even I who hadn't met her was surprised she'd died so suddenly, given the vividness with which Ron had invoked her. Ron broke down like a child and became inconsolable. He refused to attend the show that afternoon, which comprised a solo act by an old band playing country music. The old people dancing (those who could) seemed like a reel in slow motion. *This is madness. I don't belong here.* For long minutes I sat in this throng of the near dead and then I left to look for Ron.

"She was the only joy I had here," Ron explained. "Thelma and I arrived here the same day. It's been about a year now. We hit it off right away. Funny how that happens. She was the fun away from the pain. She'd lost a child, too. Kinda like me. When her husband passed, her other kid put her here. Last night she'd told me she wasn't feeling too good. I spent a lot of time with her. She was doing okay when I checked on her this morning. And then poof, she's gone. Who'll be my friend now?"

"Come on, Ron, you and I are friends," I said it out of sympathy, but also because I felt protective of him in an odd inexplicable way. Ron wept again. It seemed he couldn't control himself, this for a man who buried his wife and son. But, in any case, why should he control the swell of tears? Ought he? When I left his room, I was happier than when I went in, although I was ashamed it had come on the crumbling shoulder of an old man whose mental, physical and emotional vulnerabilities lay bare before me like a gaping wound.

Ron was close to making me see things other than my own tunnel would allow, a tunnel narrowing, heating up by the nanosecond until then. The day I went to his room I was seeking to console him but I'd left consoled instead. The presence of another tormented person was the perverted solace I was searching. Despite this selfishness, this dastardly feeding off his misery, I saw him as a means out of my own—a chance of sorts. I went to his room the next day. He and I didn't say a lot to each other, but I'm sure he recognized that I too was struggling with my own issues and in that we seemed to seek quietly a collective escape.

In that moment of shared space we fed from our forest to the core. The heaviest words he said to me were "You have a daughter. You don't belong here. You need

141

to get out of here as soon as you can." He said this without opening further details about his life. It was as though by closing previous chapters, we could read this one or live it free of the strains of the past, even when we knew how impossible that venture was, even when we knew how significant that chapter loomed. Because each man kept whatever burdens loomed from that past relatively unspoken, we were both able to reach across the unstained new page.

"You're a good man," Ron said on the last day I saw him alive. Two days after Thelma died, he'd not left his room. I went in there that morning to the assault of his unwashed body. The smell was strong, almost acrid. He'd refused to bathe or be bathed. At first I wanted to leave, but the comfort of the previous day kept me there. I wanted to open the windows. "Don't," he requested. So I sat in the smell. But in minutes, it wasn't that bad. Or perhaps I got used to it.

Ron looked more cheerful than I'd ever seen him. "There are sweet dreams and then there are bad dreams," he said. "Last night I had a sweet dream. I went to all places I'd ever wanted to go but couldn't. I was in Africa, too, Kojo. You were dancing and playing on a drum. I saw my family, the dead ones, there. They were all dancing too. Not badly. Not badly at all." He smiled. "We were having a meal and we were laughing. Just like old times." He coughed. "It was like they wanted me to be with them. It was like I wanted to be with them forever. Now, that's what I call a sweet dream."

"It sounds very nice. I wish I could dream them like that."

"When you go to bed tonight, think of all the people you love. Imagine them with you in the room. You will dream of them."

I wasn't convinced of his prescription, but I said I'd try it.

And when I left his room, I was so desperate I decided to try it. I thought of Afia and Mama and Papa. I even thought of Greta. But I found that my anger hadn't subsided. I had no dream. The next morning I rushed to Ron's room to confess my failure. His room was empty. Internally I had both an elation and a deflation. At last he was leaving the state of detachment and isolation, which meant I was losing him. At the same time it meant he would regain that part of himself that he needed in order to live. He wasn't in the dining room or the main hall. I went around looking for him without success. Finally I asked one of the nurses, "Have you seen Ron this morning?"

"Oh," she said. "You don't know?"

"Know what?"

"He passed last night...."

I didn't hear what she said next. All I could think of was that at the same time I lay in bed trying to make a dream, he was leaving. At the same time I lay angry he was dying.

I coughed.

For the first time since I arrived there, I felt as though it was only a matter of time, and I wasn't afraid. I thought of Ma and Pa. If they could do it, so could I.

I coughed again.

Humiliation and frustration come in different faces. Like beauty, their impact is in the eyes of the beholder.

144

Some would have looked this in the face, stared it down or laughed it off. Not me. I was smitten in a manner of speaking. Mine found and held my breath and slowly kneaded my life out of my body, or helped to do so. The day I died, just three days after Ron's death, I had dived deep into the pits of despair, humiliation and hopelessness. When Ron glimmered before me, even if dimly, I managed to slide these feelings to the side, believing that there was an opportunity of sorts, that I'd rise above the path drenched with sorrow, having tasted briefly the option of hope. When they took Ron's body away, the sense of loss deepened. I became inconsolable. For moments, I sat on the porch and stared into the day that had stolen the night. The grief offered no therapy from the impending death I could sense coming.

I left the porch and walked slowly toward my room. "How are you doing?" Nadia asked. I frowned at her, making no attempt to hide my disappointment or anger. "Take care of yourself!" she hollered.

Sure, it had been days since Afia called. I know she was on a trip abroad, but even a phone call?

I lay in bed, oblivious to everything around me. I focused on the need to find hope somewhere, anywhere. I found none. Therefore, I refocused my energies into one wish, the wish to die. I weighed suicide, afraid though of doing it. I wanted to die, but not at my own hands. But could I solicit the help of anyone else? I abandoned that line of inquiry. It was simply too selfish and uncertain under the circumstances.

So I was left with the option to live. And yet live for what? Jobless, divorced, abandoned by Afia, now Ron. The reemergence of Ron in my thoughts provided me with the confidence that I too was ready to leave. I hoped and prayed for death. The prayer went unanswered, a gaping disappointment the next morning when I woke up alive. But I noticed that I had developed a continuing cough. Like Ron. That gave me some hope that I was getting closer to him, closer to death. I went through the entire day devoid of all thought except the one I found so friendly: Death. Death. Death. No unwelcome lyrics to sing to it. I wanted it to come—grim ripper or no—to take me home, wherever home would be, or would become. *God forgive me, I am too weak.* I was restless and needed rest; I was homeless and needed a home; I was famished and needed feeding; I was alone and needed an embrace. Gripped by this wish, I hardly ate anything and it wasn't until later that I felt the stresses of hunger.

The next day I was walking with a new limp, surprisingly injected into my body like bad vaccination. I could hardly fathom its origin, but I welcomed it, the pain it shot up my left leg. I lived in that state of oblivion the entire day. "I'm getting worried about you," Nadia said.

"Worry about things you can change."

"How do you mean?"

"How do you mean?"

"You've not been eating."

"I'll eat when you get me some booze."

"That's out of the question."

"Then leave me alone."

"I promised Afia I'd take care of you."

"Are you my mother?"

"What kind of attitude is this?"

"Leave me alone."

She left cursing under her breath. I felt triumphant.

I didn't leave my room the next day. Nadia brought me food and insisted, "I'm not leaving until you eat."

I neither spoke nor touched the food. She sat and stared at me. I went to sleep. When I woke up she'd left, leaving a note that she'd be checking on me. I looked at the food. I had an appetite bigger than I'd have imagined, but I resisted. I broke the food into pieces and poured the boluses into the trash. When she came back, she saw what I'd done and severely tongue-lashed me. "You keep on like this and I'm going to have to force feed you."

I died that night.

I was looking down at my body lying on the bed—asleep, for a while bereft of dreams. It seemed to have aged significantly in the weeks it had been at the nursing home, or resort if that's what Afia preferred. If Afia's goal was to refurbish me, she'd failed.

I had a dream. In the dream, I had aged even more, my face wrinkled, my body withered. I was still in the nursing home, which was empty except for me. Afia came to visit me, bringing a box of chocolates. She sat beside me and made small talk, smiling at me, but her smile was hollow. It was pitiful rather than hopeful, pity expressed at the caricature I had become, the living dead her father was. She wanted to cry, hoped to reverse time so she could see me like she wanted me to be. My voice was soft and sounded forced. She had moved from town, she said. In her voice I sensed anguish, a wish, a regret. Afia left me with the box of chocolates. I took one piece and sucked on it. I couldn't chew on it because I had lost all my teeth. Someone I didn't recognize came after Afia left. He did no better than Afia's farcical attempt to cover the pity. The only pleasure I derived from his visit was that he shared Afia's box of chocolates with me. As he left I wanted to get up from the bed and follow him, borrow his body for a few minutes so I could possess the joy of youth again. But he had paid his dues to me for a few minutes and he hurried away to increase the distance between what he was and what he could become.

I was left alone again. It was hard for me to move my body, but for this last gallant deed, I must. Slowly I disrobed and with every aching limb, I hardened my resolve. When they found me, I wanted them to see me naked. With my pants in hand, I left the bed as the pain intensified. Still struggling with the pain (but now it was only pain of body), I moved my chair to the middle of the room. I was almost passing out with pain when I tied one end of my pants to the fan and the other to my neck. I was ready, standing on the chair. Then with one last effort, I kicked the chair and then my body struggled and was still. I saw Greta and Afia again and I was shamed by my wishes to leave them. Suddenly I wanted to live. I had to live. There was always hope…

The dream ended.

As the dream ended, my body eased into its death, gasping briefly for air. But death came. It came at the moment when my ex-wife had just found bodily pleasures at the hands of another man. It came at the time when my daughter was away consulting abroad and, in the business of the moment, forgot to check on me, believing me in the good hands of her friend Nadia. It was the most lonesome moment. And yet it had the broadest impact. When a celebrity dies the nation(s) mourns. I was no celebrity, therefore, I'd find no international mourning. But when an unsung individual dies, a family mourns. Therefore, my family of family and friends mourned.

So I looked at the stiffened body, dead—as if in the end all we are underneath the clothes is the unshorn, naked self as powerful as it is ugly, as frail as it is beautiful. The postmortem... seeing the head that had held so may negative thoughts, that had at times hated people and ideas, that had at times held noble and heroic ideas; the eyes that witnessed the beauty of Greta, her joys and frustration, but perhaps had failed to see beyond that, failed to see where her frustrations may have led her where I could have stopped her if I had seen; the arms that had embraced Afia and brought her to my chest to feel the heart beating with love that knows no embarrassment in the end, gives all that is antonymous with hatred, knowing that the better part that a parent produces will, or must, find its own way.

CHAPTER NINE

***

Random Visitations and Thoughts

When Celeste and I moved to Boston, I noticed a growing African immigrant population in the area. At first, I'd taken for granted that I was almost alone in Boston, that immigrants like me were few and far between. But in no time, I ran more frequently into them—at gas stations, in stores, at restaurants. There was almost always identification of the otherness (or in this case sameness?), as if we were preprogrammed to recognize one another, no matter how long we'd stayed in the US. More frequently, we'd make eye contact and then the short hesitation before the "Hi, where are you from?"

Now, that's a heavy question. The obvious intention was clear: Which part of the African continent are you from? But that belied in great measure the often long years of absence from the continent. Could anyone genuinely and properly claim to be from there no matter how long they'd left it? Could not such a person legitimately claim to be from the US? After all, if settlers in parts of the lands they conquered felt entitled to it and willed their conquered territories to themselves and their progeny, couldn't those who'd done it by settlement short of violence do the same? So how could I be surprised at those whose accents I could detect (be they West African, East African...) but would say, "I'm from Boston." One young lady in particular stared at me a long time as if I was insane to ask her, then in an accent that could easily have been Ghanaian said, "I'm from Chicago." Fair enough. I moved on.

But not when I met Olu. He walked to me at a grocery store where I'd gone to pick up some eggs. "Brother, you look like an African. Am I right?"

"Indeed."

"Olu. I'm from Nigeria."

"Kofi. Ghana."

"Ghana? We're brothers, you know, Ghana and Nigeria."

We exchanged phone numbers. I'd done that on many occasions and didn't intend to call him. Often, I didn't receive any phone calls either. Olu called, however, within the week. Did I want to get a drink after work on Friday? Why not? It wasn't as if I was going to rush home to a wild night of passionate sex with Celeste. We met at a Nigerian ran bar that Friday. To juju, soukous, and highlife music, Olu recounted his story over a few bottles of beer. He'd arrived in the US some fifteen years earlier. He'd studied journalism, earned his masters and attempted to start an African magazine. The first few weeks had been promising. "I spoke with a lot of Africans who promised their support. But that was it. They supported it with their mouths only." Olu's dream of an African magazine to fill the void he saw in US journalism never materialized. Although he managed to publish four issues, sales were poor. "I had heard a call in the African community," he explained. "Everywhere I went, I heard my fellow Africans say that American coverage of Africa was poor, at best. They only saw Africa deprived, gun toting, starved, un-dynamic, stuck, naked, painted faced, Tarzan-like. As you and I know that is not a fair depiction of the continent. Without hiding its flaws, I wanted to present a more balanced picture, stories of the Africa that is vibrant. I tried to organize fundraisers. Only a handful of Africans showed up. Can you believe there were more Americans there than Africans?"

Olu's frustration was contained, but I could detect that it was nearing despair. "I still have hope, though," he said. He had to. Without hope, what else was left? As it were, he had suspended his dream to work as a taxi driver, trying to save enough money, delaying marriage. I'd have thought a man with a master's degree and his level of intelligence would do something else. "It's not easy, my brother," he said. And no one could second that better than I.

He invited me to his apartment now and again, feeding me *egusi* soup and *fufu* or *egbono* soup and *gari*. It was through Olu that I got to know a cross section of

African immigrants in Boston. For the most part, they each seemed to harbor a dream about to happen. Many would lecture me of their goals and some were so enthusiastic they almost convinced me they'd have succeeded the next time we met. But no such luck. In the meantime, they worked menial jobs (even the most highly educated), from taxi driving to performing janitorial duties. Occasionally, I'd meet a few who'd realized or almost realized their goals – a doctor here, an engineer there. But even they, in most cases, had a story to tell. Almost invariably, they indicated that they had been short-changed somehow, that they hadn't fulfilled fully their promise. These Africans gave me the impression of a dream marking time, waiting for the appropriate time to materialize. And in many instances, after I heard a story of an as yet unfulfilled ambition, I left more sorrowful than before.

But not as perturbed when we visited Cheryl.

Cheryl put out her hand when we arrived, then pulled me toward her and embraced me. Expecting formality, her sudden warmth surprised me. The formality was a buffer we'd developed, she and I—a buffer designed to prevent our relationship from deteriorating to the point where it could impact those around us. But by extending her body into the buffer that until then was symbolized by weak handshakes, Cheryl was usurping the rules, breaching its sacred, if tacit, vows. I was uncomfortable with it, mostly because I wasn't prepared for it. Cheryl then turned to Celeste and hugged her for long seconds. "I'm *so* glad you could come," Cheryl said. She moved a step back and smiled at us. We handed her a bottle of chardonnay we'd picked up on the way.

"Thanks for inviting us," I said, hoping to control the awkwardness with which I'd responded to her embrace.

"Don't be silly," Cheryl said, tossing her head to the side and splaying her artificially straightened hair about her shoulders. "Come on in and meet the rest of my guests."

We stepped into the living room. It had an austere feel to it, being almost bare. Though no art connoisseur, I could tell the paintings on her wall were classy and most likely expensive. How could a woman who worked in the theatre afford such paintings? (As Cheryl had said, she got into the arts, "To get some culture." She had done ballet, learned to play the piano, frequented the opera, listened almost exclusively to classical music and shunned what she termed the "backward music of the inner cities".) Cheryl introduced us to the other guests, a female friend who worked as an accountant in a Boston firm, a television executive, and a man who stood silently in the corner of the room, sipping gin and tonic and radiating an aura of power and self assuredness. "Celeste and Kofi," Cheryl said, "This is my fiancé, Steven Hayes."

(So this was it. She wanted us to meet her treasure trophy. Celeste had told me her sister was a virgin. "She's saving herself for the right man," Celeste said. I contested that. There was no way a woman of her age and looks could stay a virgin so long. It was a lie, I insisted. "I know my sister, Celeste said. "She is a virgin." Well, so be it.)

Steven smiled, his manner conveying humility laced with arrogance. He extended his hand and said, "Hi. A pleasure to meet you."

I shook his massive hand. That was Steven Hayes—massive. He had a massive baldhead, his ears were massive, his hawkish nose was long, as was his chin, which held a goatee. His massive stomach bulged slightly over his waist. He was at least six feet five inches tall and his presence seemed to project itself even beyond his mere physical existence. He seemed capable of wielding enormous power that he effortlessly held in check. "Nice to meet you," I said.

As Celeste shook his hand, Cheryl announced: "Steven and I are getting married soon."

"Congratulations," I said. But I was jealous. In a way, I was even resentful, feeling somehow cheated that Steven was getting Cheryl, that my sister-in-law was going to surrender herself to this massive man. My near-resentment was worsened by the thought that she would offer him her African virginity. I hated to think like that, but I thought it nonetheless. But what was it, really, that made me think so? Was it his skin color? A white with my sister-in-law?

"Darling," Cheryl said to Steven. "I'm going to show Celeste and Kofi around."

I was gratified to have Cheryl to ourselves. I had never felt so protective of her and, therefore, so close to her. We went around the house as she showed us her bedroom, her bathroom, her patio... I was still consumed by that jealousy and hardly paid attention. At that moment, I believed I would do anything for her; most of all rescue her from Steven by knocking the daylights out of him despite his massiveness. When she led us back to Steven, I wasn't satisfied. I needed answers. "Steven," I said without thinking. I needed to find something to say to keep from imagining him with Cheryl, to keep from imagining his lips on hers.... "Are you connected with the law?" It was a silly question but the only one I could think of at that moment.

He seemed to look at me as if amused. "No, Kofi, I'm an insurance agent." He pronounced Kofi like coffee. I resented that, although not when others did the same.

"That sounds very interesting. You must work with people a lot."

"Yes," he said, then changed topics abruptly. "Kofi, that's a Ghanaian name, isn't it?"

"Yes, Cheryl told you?"

"Yes, plus I went to school with a guy from Ghana and spent a year in Ghana in the Peace Corps."

Aha!!! So that was it. Steven was *interested* in Ghana and things Ghanaian. He must have validated Ghana for Cheryl; she was justifying for him her connections to that country, I concluded. What better way than to introduce her Ghanaian born brother-in-law?

As we were going back home, Celeste told me, "Cheryl wants to introduce Steven to Ma and Pa, but she's afraid. She's really not been in touch with Ma much of late, and she's not sure how Pa will react to Steven."

"The Cheryl I know doesn't much worry about others' opinions, not even her parents," I said.

"I guess, but Steven might."

Steven, Olu, Cheryl, Celeste... American, Nigerian, Ghanaian-born, American-born.... What a mosaic. And I had to deal with each on his or her own terms. That was the law of the land. There was no other way.

162

CHAPTER TEN

***

Rendezvous

My secretary had just retired at age sixty-five. She'd been like a mother to me. And in a way, she was—reminding me of my own. Warm, concerned, even selfless, Lara had taken care of me in many ways, covering for me at the office when I needed an excuse to pick up Adwoa or Kwabena or run from school some other errand during work hours. I could discuss everything with her without shame or reservation. When Lisa's long absences from home depressed me, she'd had a word to cheer me. That Lara was so interested in Ghana and Africa generally impressed me. "To go see the motherland," she'd say, even though her skin tone was as white as they come. The affection seemed genuine. And I got used to her as part of the job. All those mornings I'd woken up (especially on accursed Mondays) cursing myself for remaining with a job I didn't want to go to, she helped me by her sheer presence and boundless enthusiasm (which I envied on occasion) to stem the creeping drudgery. And now she had retired. Worse, her replacement was a much younger woman, whose experience paled compared to Lara's. Anna was a free spirit in a league of her own.

I resented her the moment I saw her. She'd been transferred from another division to ours and as it were I had no input in hiring her as my boss insisted she was the right person for the job. So, like it or not, she was my secretary. She walked into my office the first day of work chewing and blowing a bubble gum. "Hi ya, I'm your new secretary." My first impression: carefree, careless, frivolous, puerile, incompetent...

"Hi." I could find no other word to address her, a summation of such negativity.

She extended her hand and I held out a limp one. "We'll have fun," she said.

It took me a long time to get accustomed to her loose energy, her free spirit that zigzagged into and out of things and conversations, her non-professional mannerisms. I couldn't stand her. But in all her inadequacies, she quickly established one thing. She was loyal. When I left the office to run errands, she rephrased them to my boss in a harmless way: I had to run to an impromptu meeting or something like that. Like Lara, Anna looked out for me. In hindsight, I'm not sure if it was this shared trait with Lara that weakened my dislike or whether I knew I had no choice but to work with her.

Slowly, I resisted that urge to dislike her; not easy, considering the circumstances. It took discipline, but for my own sanity, I had to transcend her in order to like her. Six months after she started working with me, I started turning the tide. But she still seemed too different, too young, too immature to commiserate with. Unlike Lara, I couldn't tell her about Lisa and I. So while I let her into my space a little, I never brought home fires into our conversation, until one afternoon when I was pulled from a meeting. "It's an emergency," I was told. I left the room and called Anna. "It's your wife," she said. "Says she's got to run somewhere and could you pick up her mom from the airport?"

My irritation was obvious. "Shit," I said inadvertently. "Didn't you tell her I was in the middle of a meeting?"

"Did, but she insisted. Said it was an emergency."

Lisa and I had arranged that she'd pick up Adwoa and Kwabena that day as I had a late meeting. And now this. I was forced to beg myself out of the meeting, barge into my office and get my jacket. My anger still showed. "Sorry," Anna said.

"It's not your fault," I said. "Sorry if I sounded a bit rude on the phone."

"That's okay. Not a problem."

"Thanks. It's just that Lisa does these things sometimes… well, never mind."

I left it there, until two weeks later when I had to stay late at the office and asked Anna to help me. She obliged. We worked until about nine. "Thanks, Anna, I appreciate your staying."

"Not a problem," she said.

166

"Have a good night."

"Kofi," she called. "Could you do me a favor?"

"Sure. What?"

"Think you can give me a ride home. It's just that I've missed the last bus. My car is in the shop."

"Oh, sure."

I drove her home. There's a certain charm in driving in the night: radio tuned to a jazz station, the streets almost deserted, the skies dark, and the heat of tired male and female bodies so proximate. I was warming up to her even more than before. The conversation was dull, however. She said she was planning on going back to school, part time.

"Wonderful. What do you want to study?"

"Computers, maybe. But eventually want to do law school"

"Law school. You've been around lawyers. Haven't you learned your lesson?"

"Come on, can't be that bad."

How could I convince her? I said nothing to that. I pulled up in front of her apartment. "Thanks," she said. "I appreciate it." Then as she got out of the car she asked, "Want to come up for a little bit?"

That question.... I'd warmed up to her from my initial animosity, but what the question suggested was far from my mind and surprising (like discovering a stone in the middle of the road and not knowing whether it was a gem or worthless). I looked at Anna anew. Her long hair, often tied in a bun, her bangs, her hazel eyes, that fleshy pair of cheeks. She had an almost beautiful face—not bad at all, certainly above average. And she held an attractive, slim physique. But she was too young. I was fifty, she was twenty-three; still (or shall I say *therefore*) substantially appealing (though a bit too flat in front), but especially enhanced now that she'd expressed ... I'm not sure what she'd expressed except that she'd opened a door and offered me a small glimpse. But the consequences seemed too dire: the office politics that could ensue, the possible gossip....

"Thanks, but I'm just too tired."

"Perhaps another time?"

"Sure. Perhaps."

On the way back home, however, I wasn't sure I'd done the right thing—I don't mean *right* in the sense of moral correctness, but *right* in the pursuit of something desirable versus desisting from that chase. Since marriage to Lisa, I'd never failed in my determination to stay faithful. I never allowed the opportunity to present itself, knowing that my will wasn't that strong, that in aligned circumstances, my determination stood little chance against the sensation of quick passions. But, now, Anna. In any case, it was wrong, I argued to myself. Or was it? Although I was proud I'd resisted (especially since it enabled me to face Lisa with an unburdened conscience), at some level something kept pushing at me that I'd just let slip a wonderful, now irredeemable opportunity. *Live a little*, it kept saying—oh, that tiny voice of mischief.

The next day, both Anna and I pretended nothing had happened. And in a way nothing had happened, but what of that brief moment of invitation, brief but telling, brief but lush in its meaning, pregnant in its abiding anticipation, strong in its power to haunt with the possibilities it had offered? We said nothing about it, but silence meant much. Despite this stern grip it held, I thought that would be the end of it, even if in a little way I felt I'd cheated myself. But I must have underestimated its reach, for the following Friday Anna returned me to its loop. As she was leaving work she said her goodnights, to which I responded in kind, adding, "Have a wonderful weekend."

"You too," she said. "And speaking of weekends, what are you doing? Anything fun?"

"Oh... I don't know..."

"Nothing with the kids?"

"They're at my in-laws in San Fran."

"Oh, just you and the wife, then?"

"She went with them."

"You mean you're going to spend the weekend by yourself?"

"I'm afraid so."

"Oh, you poor thing."

She walked out of my office and then as though in afterthought walked back in. "Listen. Why don't you come over to my place for dinner? I'll cook you something nice. I promise."

"Anna," I said, "I m not sure that's a good idea."

"Why? I don't bite. We'll just eat and talk. That way you don't have to be by yourself all night."

I wasn't persuaded, but that voice of mischief and adventure was back with mighty force, diminishing reason. Anna must have sensed my hesitation and she seized on the opportunity my indecision presented. "Come on. I'll be ready say eight-ish. Will be expecting you." And then I took a look at her, reminded that I hadn't slept with Lisa in months—the usual rust of a long marriage. The look of Anna, the invitation ... desire swelled in me like the mischief it sought to wreak. Anna walked away, leaving me with the choice and the imagined pleasures existing in that choice.

I knew if I weighed options, I'd not go. So, deliberately, I didn't, focusing instead on the thrill of the potential than the pits of the dangers. Never mind that I was putting my marriage, my career, in potential jeopardy. What if Lisa found out? What if Anna later charged me with sexual harassment, say? Seen in the best light, I was compromising my supervisory authority over her. But did I inject these into the equation then? No. Did I weigh the potential impact of what I intended to do on my children as I showered, brushed my teeth, combed my hair? No. Did I consider the potential embarrassment in the office that an affair with Anna might bring? No. All those concerns were there, but hidden below the radar by my wish for adventure, a little bit of mischief. *Live a little.* Consequences be damned.

I arrived at Anna's door five minutes after eight with a bottle of wine.

And whatever will I had before dissolved at the moment she let me in her apartment. She'd transferred herself from a workingwoman into a sexy hostess dressed in a tight red dress without shoulder straps, her wrist adorned by bracelets in gilt. Her perfume was mild, enjoyable. *Oh Seduction, please have mercy.* "So glad you came," she said, taking my hand and leading me in. "Make yourself comfortable. Dinner will be ready in a jiffy."

While we ate, it became even clearer that we had little in common, except that we shared working space. She knew nothing of Africa, let alone Ghana (but what claim did I have to Ghana at that time, anyway?). She expressed no interest in it when I brought it up, trying to gauge the reason for her interest in me. She merely shrugged. I found little interest in her mid-western upbringing (Dayton, Ohio, to be precise). Her high school stories and prom tales didn't interest me. It sounded like something borrowed from a fairy tale, too glib for real life even though I'd lived in the US many years by then. Her singsong voice, however, made it sound like an experience worth dying for, as though I were deprived for not having lived it with her. So dinner was good to the taste, but not so much to generate interest in her as a person I would enjoy spending much time with.

(And it was only in retrospect that I realized how truly blind lust is, briefly sheltered in the quick thrill that is its oblivion. If voices and trumpets had warned me, if fire and brimstone had fallen in front of me, I wouldn't have heeded the call of dangers or reason, wed then only to the

173

thought of completing what had started. For Anna and I, it was as if we were in a journey that had to be completed, our differences a mere obstacle we had to endure and then overcome. Additionally, we were both imbibing significant amounts of wine. When she went to the kitchen and returned with dessert, she walked over to my side of the table, set the dessert down and was about to serve me when I grabbed her hand. *Oh Desire, please have mercy. Oh Desire, thy will be done.* With that prompting, she bent and pushed her lips against mine. Flesh of lips pressed against flesh of lips. I had almost forgotten how fleshy a woman's lips could feel. The kiss was as abrupt as the invitation itself. I joined in, reciprocating, heart beating, palms wet, heat rising. We were both up. It was now or never as red wine colored tongues tangoed in wine soaked saliva, and hands ventured everywhere while bodies surrendered to each other. Here was sinewy lust foraging, but I was limp, not even when her hands did all the massaging she could afford to get me excited in the one place that counted. It was no good. "I just can't do this," I acknowledged the defeat.

"It's okay," she said. But what she must have been thinking: He's impotent. No wonder he's having problems with his wife.

No, Anna, I'm not impotent. I have no problem summoning the blood into my penile veins when Lisa obliges me with her body in bed. I don't know why this is happening. But would she have believed me if I told her? I didn't think so. And saying it would only seem like a desperate excuse. I said nothing in defense, therefore. I went home with some shame, but a great deal more of relief.

I was suddenly regretful that I'd betrayed Lisa. The next Monday I avoided Anna at work as much as I could, but I couldn't do so forever. There was tension, which I didn't know how to handle. She, however, seemed not troubled by it. But, for me, only time eased that tension, seeming to cement a secret between us. I knew I couldn't deny Anna anything from then on—good reviews, time off, recommendation for a raise. I did my best to please her. Luckily for me, she left the company a few months later to return to school fulltime.

Phew.

CHAPTER ELEVEN

***

Of Friends and Secrets

As the years passed, I became even more jealous of Dawn— her success at work, say. It seemed lonely where I stood. One night I drove to my friend Ralph's house, looking for some solace. I walked to the building and rang the doorbell, not knowing what I'd tell him; nor would I be capable anyway of formulating anything intelligible. I must have been led to that house by the memories that deserted me as much as they became my uninvited guide, urging me to places once familiar, places where those memories must have sought rejuvenation.

A blonde woman opened the door. She shut it. *Who is she?* A larger man opened the door moments later. "Can I help you?"

Who are you?

"I'm looking for Ralph."

"Ralph Jordan?"

"Yes."

"He left town years ago."

The memory of a desperate man, how reliable. The memory of Ralph's departure with his wife Jenny now returned with prodigal shame. (I now told myself I must not have forgotten, just wished against reality to see something of his, something familiar.) I recalled that day when I'd seen him fly off, a gleaming smile on his face. "Headed for sunny weather," he said. Who could blame him? Born and raised in Evanston, Illinois where snow is a long feature of the weather landscape, he'd gotten tired of it, bemoaning "The long winters and the short summers." He'd applied to a law firm in Los Angeles and waited only three weeks to receive the offer. Dawn, Ralph, Jenny and I had gone out to celebrate.

Over the years, I'd watched Dawn transfer some of her hopes in me to Ralph. He'd become her mentor (in a way) as they worked in the same firm and he was a few years ahead of her. (Dawn, who'd followed me to law school, now seemed disappointed in me because I hadn't become partner?). Once they entered the law firm, Ralph and Dawn shared that common drive to rise in it, and family wouldn't stand in the way, nor, in Dawn's case, race or gender. Ralph, like Dawn, sacrificed hours and hours of family life to stay in the office. Tired when she returned, Dawn would shower, read to the children (Ben, Mike and Sue)—if she wasn't too exhausted and they weren't already asleep—and fall asleep. Ralph *did this, Ralph did that*, was a constant chorus. Ralph *will make partner* became her inspiring mantra, couched in the attractive features of ambition (which, in my supposed capitulation, meant a deplumed lawyer adrift on a meaningless boat). I'd be lucky to get my wish when I'd suggest we do something on weekends. "Ralph says there's a couple of partners getting together this afternoon." (For "afternoon," substitute "night" or even "morning," as the case may be). "This is an opportunity for me to get to talk with the partners. Internal networking. Ralph says it's important. Can't miss it." I went along to those firm gatherings involving spouses, smiled and did my dutiful ass-kissing on Dawn's behalf.

179

But that wasn't enough. To plan for partnership meant other things as well, not just long hours. Dawn had to win clients and establish herself in the community as a legal expert. She volunteered to teach seminars, give speeches on aspects of her practice areas, and joined a number of civic organizations. Though she took it without complaining, and even seemed to strive, it was painful to see her struggle to juggle everything. But I wouldn't dare stand in her way. I excused myself from her way, so to speak. Needless to say, I wasn't happy during those years that dawn struggled to make partner.

I believe our sex life started its swan song during that time. Where would she find the energy, anyway? By the time she got home, she'd given emotionally, mentally and physically and sought support, not another request to expend energy, even if it had residual rewards that are hard to quantify. I learned then not to expect too much, training myself on sexual discipline.

I was somewhat Jealous of Ralph, knowing that Dawn spent more time in closer proximity to him than me.

180

To look past appearances, I often wondered how Ralph and Jenny Jordan managed to keep their marriage intact. They had no children. That may have helped. But Jenny's stoicism (or was it just a façade?) astonished me. I took the least opportunity to exhume my frustration to her when we were left by ourselves in many law firm functions when Ralph and Dawn mingled with partners. Jenny would tell me how proud she was of Ralph. "He's going to make it," she'd say.

Proud of this? Proud of a life bereft of purpose except this unwavering drive to become partner in a law firm? A life devoid of the usual—or was it usual to the participants?—need for leisurely evenings spent underneath darkening skies, evenings seized with promenades in avenues under green leafed trees and singing birds, evenings of love-making and more love-making in the mornings, or days taken off work to commiserate and plan for a future of old age…. Listening to Jenny, I wondered if she was an anchor or just a serenading voice, whether Ralph had some supernatural strength. How did he do it?

My jealousy waned only when I recalled, under the influence of liquor, Ralph's confession to me one day when I told him, almost in tears, that he had it all while I seemed to be marking time. He told me never to envy anyone, although he too confessed that he envied us—Dawn and me and our kids. And, as if relying on the cushion of our close relationship in since our law school days, he painted a picture for me. In it, I saw Ralph and Jenny ease out of their Saturday morning sheets, unsoiled by semen, almost unruffled except for the double impressions of their bodies where they'd slept. She kissed him quickly on the cheek. It aroused him and he wanted her that very moment and hoped to succeed where he'd failed many times. He began by turning her face so he could see her and then he kissed her on the lips again and again before forcing his tongue into her mouth, but he did all the kissing. Then he pulled back and roamed her with his tongue. His hands joined his tiring tongue, working and working. Not once did she express the moan his heightened senses wanted to hear. Thirty minutes later (too long for foreplay in my estimation), he was exhausted from the effort, but his need was still evident in its throbbing concreteness. He mounted her. She closed her eyes. He entered, but found her dry. He withdrew, regretfully. "It's no good," he said.

"I'm sorry," she said.

"It's okay, hon."

His desire for her raged still, doubling the regret in the hard fact of their failed love-making. He remembered the days of courtship, when he'd kiss her and then attempt to go further and she'd say, "Not before marriage, Ralph."

He remembered the night of their wedding when full of champagne, he'd hoped to build the night into a memory she'd forever cherish. And for that reason, he'd taken his time. But at the moment of consummation he sensed her hesitation, almost an apprehension. More than anything that wedding night, Ralph wanted his wife to remember this first act of their physical love. Because he wasn't sure, he tried again and again. Masked in his wishes and the liquor he'd drunk, he was unable to fathom what he was facing until the next day when sober he re-embarked on his attempt to give her the full joy he believed she deserved. At least, in the beginning, she'd tried to get there for him. And failed. Eventually, he'd attempt it less and less, traveling that path only when the desire was too strong to bear alone.

As he dismounted her, he still had his hardness. He kissed her lightly and said, "I'll go take a shower." He went to the bathroom, turned on the shower so it was gushing, took hold of, and massaged, himself to climax. As he did that he cursed this dilemma-curse: he was blessed with a wife nearly perfect, but with whom he couldn't share this basic desire. Because she seemed to take it in pain, he was reluctant to attempt it. I am married, he said, why must my life be one masturbatory act after another?

When Ralph returned to the bedroom, she'd left it. The bed was made and no sign of his form existed on it, not even the imagined thought of the closeness over the night had any physical manifestation at the moment. He dressed and joined her in the kitchen. He explained that he'd volunteered to help clean up some homes for indigents under his law firm's auspices. Once he left, as she later confessed to him, she was relieved and burdened at once. After each failure to give all of herself to him, she accused herself anew, guilty that she couldn't overcome the three demons of years before. She wanted distance between them. The relief offered by his absences allowed her minutes of self-reclamation. By the time he returned, she was her usual self and together they saw a movie that night, in which Ralph's frustration was transferred into the affection he felt on the day they first met. Only it was a bit stronger now given the riddle she had presented him that made her seem so vulnerable in his hands, yet so unreachable. He put his hand around her shoulders.

It was this affection beyond the physical frustration that followed them wherever they went. This affection was what others saw and felt. It was what I felt on those occasions when I saw them together at functions. What I didn't see then were Ralph's ways of reaching sexual satisfaction and the occasional moments he cursed his life for taking this turn. Nor did I see then the moments when Jenny lay deep into the night in wakeful worry over her lack of children, sometimes accompanied by tears, so that

185

Ralph had to comfort her to sleep. But like her past that impacted the present, she rarely spoke of this deep desire to her husband (who was at best ambivalent about having children), perhaps fearing that to broach the matter often would mean confronting too frontally the demons she could not be sure she could fight successfully. Paradoxes and complications. In the end, like Siamese twins who wouldn't be able to live apart, Ralph and Jenny's departure to Los Angeles was as much a desire to seek warmer climates as to find a new beginning that would keep them together; conjoined still, perhaps renewed.

Yet when the man closed the door in my face, I did not immediately bring this to bear such barricade of information and knowledge to mount against the irk over what seemed Ralph's abandonment. With law school winding down, me looking for a job, he'd said, "Let's stay here, man. Not a bad place to start a career." I'd listened, although my intention was to go to Washington DC. And most of my interviews were with DC law firms. But in hindsight, I was thankful for the couple of Chicago law firms I put on the interview list at the last minute. One of them would give me a job offer.

In law school, Ralph had lived a couple of blocks from me. As we walked home sometimes, he lamented the rigors of law school (I shared the lament); he expressed his desire to leave law school (I did too); he bemoaned the facelessness of the process (I concurred in the analysis that led to that conclusion); and he stated his remorse at not having enough time to relax (I agreed with that)...

Memories of law school days...

"Hey, Jenny, me and a couple of my friends are getting together tonight. Maybe go downtown, have dinner and get some drinks later on. Want to join us?" I made an excuse. "Well, if you change your mind, let me know." I didn't.

Freeze frame. I had embraced his friendship without question but I attempted to dodge his friendship on occasion. Not that I disliked him. Far, far from that. I liked him—that infectious easygoing manner, that generous spirit. And yet he seemed far too fun loving and carefree.

Plus, even in his company, I was beginning to feel as if I remained an experiment in the complex laboratory of racial disharmony and personal attempts at its correction. I felt that too many times I had been burned by such an experiment gone awry—just because I'd been the only black around when an offhand comment (or perhaps it wasn't offhand) seemed so awful. Like the day in college when I'd gone with two fraternity boys to a frat party and someone had said, "Man, there's this big, ugly *black* chick on my floor who's so fucking into herself she won't talk to anyone else on the floor." He turned to me and said, "No offense intended." Why he would pick that time and topic was beyond me…. Or that day when I'd gone to see a movie at the invitation of a white friend and a black man had asked a white man "…or do you hate niggers?" And the response had come, "I hate niggers," and the audience had applauded. And my friend had gasped. And I had wondered if he would have clapped with the rest if I weren't sitting next to him….

But in Ralph I couldn't detect the reserve I found in so many others. I never had, but I became more experienced, more cautious, more judgmental, given the thick lenses of my years living in the country. I hated doing it, but it was as if I was asking him to re-justify his friendship. I tried to gauge him anew with questions, listen carefully to what he said. I found nothing suspicious. It hadn't always been like that for me.

When I first arrived in the US to attend college, I was open like an unwritten book, moldable. I could embrace anyone. Anyone. I had no historical, experiential, mental or emotional gauge for determining who would be or not be my friend in my new found land. Race as a determining condition was remote to that as yet unformed gauge. My hand was out. Hold it, anyone. Hold it and be my friend. Ralph had held it, and can anyone ask more of another? But because my hands were darker than others, some accepted and some rejected it. Of course, rejection is rarely outright—I had to see it as subtle as the cold winter wind sifting through underneath the bolted door, a subtle alienation that requires all the instincts of experience or history to detect. Yes, to experience is to learn. To have a heart is to fear its abuse and therefore to develop coping mechanisms. But finding no negative in Ralph (at least as yet), I would find the hand and we would be friends. Years later, I was no longer as open as before. I too learned to watch carefully. My education had not been in the classroom only.

CHAPTER TWELVE

***

The Return

I see the family home standing sturdy after all these years, but in need of repair, its walls battered by rain and scorched by sun. Beaten, but standing; frail, but standing; shaken, but standing.

Oh, ancestral land, I am so proud of the way you still stand proud despite the corrosive battering of the years.

Inside, my brother Kofi is retiring after a hard day, tired as he rests on the bed, his arms folded over his belly as his wife finishes the chores outside. Soon, she'll join him. It has been weeks since he got word that I was dead. My eldest brother had not known what to feel when he heard the news. It was that calculated a reaction, going first through the mind. I hadn't seen him in years. And I was almost a stranger to him. But a brother is a brother and a loss is a loss, although this felt like the way you'd feel at the death of a celebrity you'd never met, but liked—none of that seizure of grief that rocks the core of one's self, none of that pulsating sense of doom, none of the suffocating feeling of helplessness.

Just an ache in a newly created void. What a tragedy, he had said. But the tragedy to him was not the death itself, but the lost opportunity to know me as I got older, to know my children, my wife, and *vice versa*. The brief encounters with his nephews and sister-in-law were inadequate, simply too brief to forge bonds. To him, the tragedy lay in my forever lost place in the family tree, a blank where a living being used to be, albeit in absentia. But also, a reminder of the inevitability of death, which rocked him more than Papa's or Mama's death. I was closest to him in age; therefore, he became more aware of his vulnerability to mortality, which added a bit of anger to the loss.

Kofi had given the news to my sisters Yaayaa and Akosua the way a man would pass an unwanted legacy to

192

his kin. As though to berate him for his calm, they began to wail immediately. He in return seemed irked by the outburst and turned his back on them and went indoors. My brother Kwabena heard the wailing and hurried to my sisters to investigate. When he heard that I had died, he joined his sisters in the wailing. Now the entire family was roused to find out what was happening: My brother Kofi's children Owusu and Akoto, Yaayaa's husband Osei, and her children Nsiah and Adom, and Kwabena's wife Serwaah and their child Anane. The notable absence was Akosua's husband, who'd left her for another woman.

The unity I hadn't achieved in life I did in death. The entire family (at least those living in the family home) had gathered over the news. This was the first since Papa and Mama's death. A blessing, they believed, that all the children born into the home had lived. But Kofi stayed inside his room the rest of the day, mostly because he wished not face the ringing misery of the rest of the family. How do you mourn a man you no longer know? He was shamed by it, but found that he couldn't feel the deep pain that he wanted. And yet he'd been my closest brother before I left Ghana. He was only three years older and, therefore, almost my age. My sister Yaayaa was six years younger, Ama eight years younger, and Kwabena eleven years younger.

In my ghostly visit, I saw the young ones I'd only seen in pictures. There was Kwabena's son Anane staring at his father, his aunts, knowing that Uncle Kofi had died, but not knowing how to react. The knife wound on his thigh he'd accidentally self-inflicted the previous day was more real to him than the death being mourned, the death of an unknown man he'd seen in pictures who lived in America and who he expected would one day return with great gifts. Little Anane looked on a little amused by the level of the weeping, its loudness. He'd never seen his aunts cry so loudly and now he felt some sympathy for them. He, too, liked to break open from time to time.

Perhaps it was empathy he felt. But the hardest decision he had to make immediately was whether to cry. When he saw his father cry as well, he knew he'd be in the wrong unless he did likewise. Little Anane needed something to spur him to tears, though. Not finding anything, he hit his injured knee. *Brave child; but why waste your tears, little one?* The pain made him wince, but not cry. His wound started bleeding, however. It was only when he saw the blood oozing from the wound that he began crying. Tears at the sight of blood. His father saw him standing by himself crying. And not just the sight of his son in tears, but also the gushing sense of protection washing over him (in view of the news of my death), prompted Kwabena to pick up his son and console the young one.

The natural course of events—memory recedes, pain subsides, and life must continue.

Printed in the United States
By Bookmasters